OTHER
Harlequin Romances
by ROSEMARY POLLOCK

SONG ABOVE THE CLOUDS

by

ROSEMARY POLLOCK

HARLEQUIN BOOKS

TORONTO
WINNIPEG

Original hard cover edition published in 1972
by Mills & Boon Limited, 17-19 Foley Street,
London W1A 1DR, England

© Rosemary Pollock 1972

SBN 373-1675-1

Harlequin edition published April 1973

Printed in Canada

1675

CHAPTER ONE

CANDY shivered, and tightened the belt of her rain-coat. The steady drizzle that for the last half hour had been falling with relentless persistence from an uncompromisingly grey sky seemed, if anything, to be getting worse. Her hair was soaked already, for she hadn't had the forethought to bring a headscarf with her, and she had just made the discovery that her brand new shoes could not by any stretch of the imagination be described as water-tight. It occurred to her that if either she or Sue or both of them were going to have to go in search of help it would be just as well if they did so fairly quickly, for it was already well past five o'clock, and the autumn evening was beginning to close in. Before very long it would be dark. But Sue's neat, trouser-suited form had almost disappeared beneath the bonnet of the Vauxhall, and Candy was determined not to seem impatient. Sue, she knew quite well, was already pretty badly upset.

If only they hadn't gone out of their way in order to have tea at the Star and Crossbow they might by now have been running smoothly into the West End of London, in nice time for their rendezvous—or rather, Candy's rendezvous—with Signor Caspelli. But they had gone out of their way, and as a result Sue's car had decided to break down in what seemed to be one of the loneliest and least-used byways in the whole of Southern

England. They had been marooned there now for nearly three-quarters of an hour, and in the whole of that time the only being to go past along the road had been a wandering and lugubrious-looking Ayrshire cow. If Candy hadn't been quite so cold and wet the whole situation would have struck her as being ridiculously funny, and even as it was she couldn't bring herself to feel nearly as fed-up as she knew Sue must be feeling. Perhaps it was a pity about Signor Caspelli, but it couldn't be helped. It was just one of those things.

Sue emerged from under the bonnet, and straightened herself. Her face was damp with perspiration, as well as rain, and her beautifully manicured hands were black.

"It's no good—the wretched thing won't go." She pushed her hair back, streaking her forehead with grease, and looked at her watch. "I'm sorry, Candy. It's *awful*."

"Of course it isn't awful." Candy smiled at her. "Signor Caspelli can wait. He'll probably agree to see me in the morning; he isn't leaving for New York until tomorrow afternoon."

"But would he give you another chance? I mean, people hate broken appointments. . . ."

"Well, if he won't, he won't. But anyway, Sue, it isn't the end of the world. Really! Don't look so shattered. Let's set out to walk, and see if we can find a telephone or something."

Reluctantly, Sue closed the bonnet. "All right. I think I saw a phone box about half a mile back." She sighed. "We'd better ring Paul's mother, and tell her we'll be turning up four hours earlier than expected. There's just one lucky thing about this situation, and that's the fact that Great Mincham can't be more than five or six miles away."

They closed and locked the Vauxhall's doors and windows, and Sue wiped her greasy hands on an insubstantial handkerchief, then they started to walk back down the lane in the direction of the telephone box—which Candy devoutly hoped had not been a figment of Sue's imagination. She also hoped that Sue's mother-in-law would not be too upset at the prospect of having to receive her guests in time for dinner when she had been expecting to receive them in time for bed...a point which certainly wouldn't be likely to worry Sue herself, but did worry Candy. It really worried her quite as much as the knowledge that she, an aspiring young singer, had just missed an audition with one of the world's leading operatic impresarios.

As she picked her way round rather a large puddle, and tried to forget about the mud already squelching between her toes, she decided that there must be something basically wrong with her. She couldn't feel disappointed about the audition—not if she tried. In an odd sort of way, she even felt relieved. It might have been fun to be taken on by the great Caspelli, but she wouldn't have been good enough, and the whole thing would have been sheer humiliation. She was certain of that. The girl selected by the famous Italian would be boosted internationally as an exciting new musical discovery, she would sing in Paris and Vienna, New York and Rome—and she would have to bear comparison with all the leading sopranos of the modern world. The idea that she, Candy Wells, could ever have stood a chance of becoming that girl was really, when she came

7

to think about it, quite ridiculous. She didn't even know that she would have wanted to become that girl.

"I think I'm glad I missed the audition," she told Sue suddenly. "I really would have looked an idiot— competing with all those brilliant young hopefuls. After all, I've little or no stage experience, and since I left school I haven't even had any proper training. I'd probably have struck Signor Caspelli as a huge joke."

"That's rubbish!" said Sue crisply. "You've got a voice like an angel. Even Paul thinks so, and he's not exactly musical." She managed a slight laugh. "I've made up my mind that you're going to have your chance—and you will have it, even if I find it necessary to waylay this Caspelli man personally!"

Candy bent her head as the rain grew heavier, and smiled a little whimsically. "I think you're trying to turn me into something I'm not."

"I'm trying to turn you into what you really are." Sue sounded a little grim. "You've wasted three years already, and it's my fault. Out there in Hong Kong, with Paul, I didn't give you a thought—not a serious thought, I mean. That's honest, and it's high time I was honest! You wrote and told me you'd got a job in a West End flower shop, and I just thought 'how nice'. It's true I imagined you would be going ahead with your singing at the same time, but I never even asked you, did I?"

Candy felt embarrassed. Her sister's orgy of self-criticism had lasted almost from the moment of her arrival at Heathrow Airport three weeks before, and apparently it hadn't exhausted itself yet.

8

"Don't be silly," she said. "Look, there's the main road. I think I can see your call-box."

"Thank goodness for that! We'll ring the Caspelli man first, and then Paul's mother."

But when they got to the telephone box and pooled their resources they made the discovery that they only had enough change of the right sort for one call—and that call, naturally, had to be to Sue's mother-in-law. Candy waited outside while her sister telephoned, for the rain was easing off a little, and it struck her that when Sue re-emerged she was looking slightly more satisfied with life.

"Alison's handling everything," she said. Sue's mother-in-law preferred to be known by her Christian name. "She's getting on to a garage about the car, and Paul's father's coming over for us. I told you it wasn't far, didn't I?" She hesitated, then added slowly: "We're not the only visitors they're expecting to-night. John's just back from Rome. He's coming down to Mincham for the week-end."

If she had expected this information to have some noticeable effect on her sister, she wasn't disappointed. Quite unmistakably, Candy's eyes lit. "You mean... John will be there to-night?"

"Well, I suppose so, unless he's like us, and has a breakdown." She added casually: "Did you know he was back? I'm sure Paul doesn't."

Candy shook her head. "No, I didn't know." He must have been planning to surprise her; that was typical of John. Under Sue's interested gaze she actually smiled, rather idiotically, as she thought of him. He had probably forgotten that she would be on holiday in

9

Lincolnshire, staying with Sue, and when he got back from Rome he would have called at the flower shop, as he always did, at closing time, only to discover that she wasn't there. As a leading producer of television documentaries he travelled a good deal, and every time he arrived back in London the first thing he seemed to do was call at the flower shop.

They got on well together, she and John. Wonderfully well, in fact. Ever since the day, four years earlier, when Sue had married Paul Ryland she, Candy, had somehow known that Paul's elder brother was going to occupy a special place in her life, and from that day onwards an extraordinary bond had developed between them. It was true that there was a big gap between their ages—when they met she had been seventeen and he had been thirty-four—and she supposed it should have created some kind of barrier. But it had never seemed to worry John, and it certainly didn't worry her. She had taken to him, on Sue's wedding day, not only because he was tall and dark and looked shattering in morning dress but because he was kind, and although he was best man and she was chief bridesmaid didn't seem to feel the smallest urge to tease her. When her first glass of champagne threatened to choke her he had saved her from public humiliation by emptying it into a flower pot and surreptitiously refilling it with lemonade, and afterwards he had talked to her about music, which at that time had been the most important thing in her life. A year later her father had died—her mother had died when Candy was still a child—and to the astonishment of everyone but his bank manager and his solicitor Robert Wells had left nothing whatsover behind him but a terrifying stack of debts. The double shock had descended on Candy with the force of a landslide, and if John hadn't been on hand to advise her she didn't really know what she would have done. Sue had been with her husband in Hong Kong, caught up by a multitude of fascinating new interests, and the reality of what was happening at home in England hadn't quite seemed to get through to her. There were no other relatives to turn to, and as her father's house and possessions were sold and the world rocked around her John had been the only person she had felt able to discuss things with.

Her singing, which she loved so much, had been abandoned—John had agreed that for the time being it was unavoidable—and he had found her the flower shop job. The shop was run by a friend of his, a Mrs. Cheyney, and because it was pleasant and secure Candy had accepted the job with grateful eagerness, and had clung to it ever since. As for her relationship with John. . . . In theory it had remained nothing more than a particularly important and long-lasting friendship, but in reality it was a very long time since Candy had been able to think of Sue's brother-in-law as just a friend. And although he rarely said or did anything to indicate that he thought of her as anything other than a kind of younger sister she knew she was important to him. Having waited such a long time already, he was naturally not in a hurry to get married. Where she was concerned he would be cautious—as much, she suspected, for her sake as for his own. But for ages now she had been unable to imagine a future that didn't include John. He was like a rock—the best and most dependable thing in her life—and she was happily confident that, whatever happened, he would always be there. And perhaps one day—one day, if she were patient—she would occupy a more important place in his life. A *really* important place.

The rain had stopped, and in pale, fitful sunshine they wandered up and down, waiting for the arrival of Sue's father-in-law. Candy looked happily abstracted, and it was obvious that all thought of the missed audition had been banished completely from her mind. Watching her, Sue wondered what there really was between her and John. Almost from the day the two of them met she had been out of the country, and she didn't know.

"I'm going to ring Caspelli," she said. "And if I've any powers of persuasion left, you'll be getting that audition to-morrow morning."

Candy smiled at her. "I ought to ring...."

"Well, you're not going to." Their hostess, having emerged for a moment or two to kiss her daughter-in-law and commiserate rather vaguely with Candy had disappeared again, and the two girls were alone. "For one thing," Sue went on, "you wouldn't even try to get another appointment. I know you! Alison did say which room you were having, but if you'd rather just wait in the drawing-room while I'm phoning...you know where it is, don't you?"

Candy nodded. "Yes." And then she hesitated for a moment. "Don't try too hard, Sue. It isn't worth it."

And even if it had been worth it, she thought privately, the chances of anyone's inducing the great Caspelli to give a second chance to an unknown girl who had already missed one audition were so slight as to be barely worth considering. Sue would put up a fight—that went without saying, for the whole thing had been Sue's idea. If she hadn't read in the newspapers about Signor Caspelli's search for a brilliant new soprano voice and immediately decided that her younger sister was what he was looking for Candy would never even have thought of putting her own voice forward. Sue would fight to the bitter end—but it wouldn't come to anything, and in a way that was rather a relief.

A singing career would take her out of the safe haven of Mrs. Cheyney's flower shop and into the world, and Candy wasn't at all sure she was ready for that. She wasn't sure she ever would be ready for it.

As she made her way along a thickly carpeted corridor in the direction of Alison Ryland's drawing-room she stopped in front of a little gilt-framed looking-glass and took a comb out of her handbag. The face that looked back at her was small and oval, with high cheekbones and a suggestion of porcelain delicacy about the pretty mouth and the neat, straight nose. But it was her wide, lustrous grey-green eyes and the thick brown lashes overhanging them that were Candy's most striking feature, and to-night the eyes looked very large, and preternaturally serious. She ran the comb through her hair—fine, golden-brown hair that curled alarmingly whenever it was allowed to get wet—and as she did so her ears caught the sound of piano music.

It was coming from the drawing-room at the end of the corridor and it wasn't, she was reasonably certain, proceeding from either a wireless set or a record player. She put the comb back in her handbag, and tried to decide whether to go on, or retreat upstairs to her own bedroom—Alison Ryland always gave her the same room, so she knew exactly where to go. She stood hesitating for several seconds, but then she heard her sister's voice—Sue was on the telephone, speaking to someone on Signor Caspelli's staff—and she knew that if she were to retrace her steps and climb the stairs she wouldn't be able to avoid hearing every word of Sue's frantic efforts on her behalf. She shook her head at her own cowardice, but walked on towards the drawing-room door.

Then, with her fingers on the door-handle, she paused again, listening. The music was Schubert in one of his more melancholy moods, subdued and deceptively simple, and the unseen pianist had an extraordinarily expressive touch. Every note was alive with an arresting sadness that struck her as almost eerie and by the time she finally pushed the door open she felt rather curious to know who it was who was responsible.

The drawing-room at the Old Rectory was long and beautiful and had been furnished with flawless taste in the style of the early Regency. Its colour scheme was a delicious blend of gold and white and dusty pink, and it had always seemed to Candy to possess the ideal atmosphere—a blissful tranquillity that made the outside world seem a thousand miles away. It was usually filled with flowers, and to-night, as she stood in the doorway looking about her, she saw that every available vase held huge shaggy chrysanthemums. And then her eyes travelled to the piano, and took in the figure of the man seated before the keyboard. He was wearing a grey suit—a very well cut grey suit—and his hair was smooth and dark brown, but that was as much as she could see, for he had his back to her, and he didn't seem to have heard her come in. She knew he was someone she had never seen before, and all at once she felt rather shy. She wanted to stay and listen to his music, but at the same time she did not want to interrupt him, or draw attention to herself.

So she closed the door behind her as quietly as she could, and for two or three minutes stood absolutely still, while the flow of gentle sound went on and on. He changed to Brahms, and then to Schumann, and as a passionate lover of almost all forms of music Candy was entranced. She wondered whether he could be a professional pianist, and she was just trying to remember whether John had ever mentioned having a friend with serious musical aspirations when the clasp of her handbag, which hadn't been properly fastened, came open with a snap, and the man at the piano stopped dead in the middle of a bar.

"Oh, I'm sorry!" Candy said involuntarily. "I mean . . . I didn't want to interrupt you."

He looked round, and then stood up. He was tall and rather slightly built, and as he turned to face her she could see that he didn't look English. He could, she decided, be French . . . even, possibly, Italian. Although neither his hair nor his eyes were strikingly dark there was an intense brownness about them that was anything but Anglo-Saxon, and there was something in his face that made her think, rather absurdly, of faces she had seen engraved on old coins—not English coins. He was quite young—somewhere in his late twenties, she supposed—and yet there was a strange kind of weariness

15

in his eyes and in the lines about his sensitive mouth that gave him almost a tragic look.

He stared at her for at least six seconds without saying a word, and then he bowed slightly.

"It's I who should apologize. Such a beautiful piano was a great temptation, but I should not have touched it without asking your mother's permission. I have not disturbed anyone?"

For a moment Candy looked bewildered, and then she shook her head, smiling a little. "Mrs. Ryland isn't my mother. I'm only staying here for the week-end. But I know she likes to hear anyone play." Hesitantly, she added : "Wouldn't you like to go on? I—I was enjoying it."

"Were you?" He still seemed to be studying her, but at the same time she got the weird impression that in reality he was staring right through her. "How long had you been listening?"

"Only two or three minutes." Suddenly she felt uncomfortable. "If you'd rather I went away...."

She seemed to have succeeded in catching his attention. "Do you want to go away?"

"No, but...." This was ridiculous, and oddly embarrassing into the bargain. "If I'm disturbing you—"

"You aren't," he said quickly. "Please stay. And if it really gives you pleasure to hear an excellent piano being abused by a very clumsy amateur I'll play anything you like." He spoke with an unmistakably alien accent, but his English was extraordinarily good. "You are fond of music?"

"Yes. I'm very fond of music."

"You play yourself, perhaps?" Candy had dropped

into a huge brocade-covered armchair, and he was once again seated at the piano.

"Only a little."

"But you appreciate the efforts of others." He smiled, and his face was transformed. "You like Chopin?"

"I think everybody likes Chopin."

"Not quite everybody." He ran his fingers lovingly over the gleaming ivory keys, and once again the room was filled with glorious sound. "But, looking at you, one can see. . . . Yes, naturally you like Chopin."

He began to play a haunting little waltz, and Candy put her head back against a pile of cushions and relaxed completely. Normally, she was apt to feel ill at ease with strangers, but somehow this foreigner, despite his abstracted manner and his melancholy eyes, didn't have that sort of effect on her. He came to the end of the waltz and embarked on a familiar nocturne, and as she listened she completely forgot about Sue, and Signor Caspelli, and everything else that should have been on her mind at that moment. She was warm, and comfortable, and the piano was infinitely soothing. . . . Reality seemed a long way away.

Then suddenly the door to the hall was thrown wide. There was a murmur of voices, and the next moment Sue appeared on the threshold. She was talking to someone who was just behind her, but when she caught sight of Candy she came forward rather quickly, and it was easy to see that she had nothing particularly pleasant to communicate.

"I'm terribly sorry, Candy—I did try, honestly, but it wasn't any good. Caspelli's secretary says he's made his choice! And anyway, the beastly man's leaving in the morning, and won't give any more auditions in London. I feel so *dreadful* about it, because it's all my fault. Darling, are you awfully upset?"

"Of course I'm not," Candy assured her truthfully. Sue's entrance had startled her a bit, partly because Signor Caspelli and the vexed question of whether or not he might be prepared to receive her had temporarily gone right out of her head. She turned to introduce their fellow guest, who had stopped playing and silently risen to his feet, but then it occurred to her that she didn't know his name, and as she hesitated she saw that somebody else had entered the room in the wake of Sue. Her cheeks flushed with pleasure, and everything else was forgotten.

"*John!*" She made no attempt to keep the naïve delight out of her voice—she couldn't have managed it, anyway. "I didn't know you'd got here yet!"

"Hello, Candy! Didn't you?"

He stood in the doorway, smiling at her rather absently. Over six feet tall, and as ruggedly handsome as a film star, John Ryland had always had an overwhelming effect on women, and in Candy's opinion at least, there was no other man in the length and breadth of the earth who could possibly bear comparison with him. This fact showed quite clearly in her face as she stood looking at him, waiting for him to come over and ask her what she had been doing with herself in the past few weeks, and to Sue, and possibly also to the other man present, the transparent eagerness in her eyes was almost painfully revealing.

But John didn't go over to her. Instead, he hurried

forward with outstretched hand to greet the man still standing beside the piano.

"Well, well, so you made it. I hope you had a decent drive down. The roads round here probably gave you a spot of trouble—they can seem a bit like a maze, sometimes."

The stranger inclined his head in a gesture that could have been thought faintly condescending. "Thank you, I had a very good journey."

"Oh, well, that's fine." John sounded relieved. He hesitated, glancing at Candy and Sue. "Has everybody met the Conte di Lucca? Or is it up to me to make the introductions?"

Candy said nothing, but Sue, viewing the attractive foreigner whom she had so far ignored with sudden keen interest, shook her neat dark head emphatically. "I haven't met anybody—I've been tied to the telephone ever since I got here." She held her hand out to the Conte, and he bowed over it, while John completed the introduction and then glanced at Candy. With a clumsy attempt at teasing, he said :

"We mustn't forget Sue's little sister."

Candy flushed, feeling oddly hurt and embarrassed. But the Conte di Lucca turned and smiled at her.

"The Signorina and I have not yet been introduced," he said. "But I would not say that we haven't met. We share a love of Chopin."

"Oh, you've been talking music, have you?" John looked mildly surprised, but he couldn't by any stretch of the imagination have been said to look resentful. He introduced them formally, and then he added : "The

Conte comes from Italy, Candy. Perhaps he'll give you some advice about your singing."

"Singing?" The Conte raised his narrow dark eyebrows.

"Yes." John glanced at his watch with the same sickening air of abstraction. "Candy's quite keen on singing." Something came back to him, and he went on : "Sue tells me she's just had a bit of a disappointment in that direction ... missed an audition or something, so she needs cheering up. I'm sorry about that, Candy, it was hard luck."

She said nothing, and he ran his hands through his thick dark hair, and looked at his watch a second time. "Well, I think I'll go and tidy up before dinner. I'll see you later, Conte—remind me to ask you about that great-uncle of yours and his archaeological interests. He should make good material."

The Italian inclined his head very slightly. John left the room, and Candy stood quite still, looking rather like a crestfallen child. The bewilderment in her face was the bewilderment of a small girl who has suddenly made the discovery that grown-ups can be quite incomprehensible at times. But the hurt just beginning to dawn in her eyes had nothing at all to do with childishness, and her sister, whose eyebrows had ascended a trifle, didn't fail to notice the fact.

"John must be absolutely flattened out after that drive down from London." Her voice, a little too bright and rallying, broke sharply into the silence that had fallen, and Candy jumped as if she had been awakened from a trance.

"Yes," she said. "He must be."

She heard Sue ask the Conte di Lucca if he were not tired, too, after his journey, but she didn't hear his answer. John—her John—had gone away from her, and this man who had come back from Rome in his place was somebody utterly different. Sue, and the Italian, and everything else around her seemed a long way away. Nothing was quite real. She felt incapable of movement, and for several minutes she remained motionless, hearing nothing and saying nothing, until at last Sue took her in hand, and bustled her off to change for dinner. The only thing she noticed, as she walked towards the door, was the look in the eyes of the Conte di Lucca as he watched her go. He had curiously expressive eyes, and at this moment they were alight with a kind of detached sympathy. She had the feeling, suddenly, that he read not only her mind but her soul, and that the pity he felt for her was the pity he might have felt for a child crying over a lost Teddy Bear. He understood her unhappiness, but for him it was very trivial.

She was glad when the door had closed behind her, and she was safe, for a time, from the cool penetration of those alert brown eyes.

CHAPTER TWO

THE dining-room at the Old Rectory was panelled in white, and in daylight its long windows looked over the splendours of an eighteenth-century rose garden on to a gentle panorama of undulating pastureland, with the squat grey tower of the little village church just visible through the branches of the elm tree beyond the orchard. Candy loved the view, as she loved everything about the house, but on this October evening long curtains of aubergine velvet had already been drawn across the windows, and the candelabra that adorned the dining-table tall candles had been lit. The room looked charming, for the thick, expensive carpet that flowed into every corner matched the curtains in colour, and the polished table was ablaze with silver and bright with flowers, but at the same time on this particular evening Candy thought it all looked a little cold and formal, and despite the central heating she shivered as she put the finishing touches to the bowl of fruit she had been arranging. For the last half hour she had been in the kitchen, helping Mrs. Ryland and her faithful 'daily' with some of the preparations—partly because she liked to be useful, and partly because she didn't feel very much like joining the chattering, aperitif-consuming party in the drawing-room. John was in there, she knew, discussing Rome with the Conte di Lucca, and Sue, elegant and sparkling in clinging emerald brocade, was in there too, but Candy had the peculiar feeling that there was no place for her amongst them, so instead she made her way to the kitchen, where Mrs. Wren, the 'daily', was basting pheasants and talking about the new Vicar, and Alison Ryland, her black velvet dinner-dress covered by an overall, was decorating an enormous gateau with cherries and whipped cream. They looked at Candy with absent-minded, indulgent smiles—thinking vaguely what a nice child she was—and found her little jobs to do, but neither of them paid any particular attention to her, and for that she was grateful. She polished glasses and filled pepper-pots and, finally, arranged the fruit. And then, just as she placed the last burnished orange in position, the little carriage clock on the mantelpiece chimed eight, followed almost immediately by the wheezing grandfather in the hall, and Mrs. Wren tore herself away from her pheasants and emerged from the kitchen to beat the gong for dinner.

Candy heard the drawing-room door open, and the sound of voices and laughter drawing nearer, and she stiffened a little as she waited by the sideboard. She was tense because so much depended on what happened when John came into the room—on what he said to her, how he looked at her. It could be that she had imagined the change in him, that she was being over-sensitive . . . or it could simply be that his trip to Italy had exhausted him in some way, that he just wasn't himself.

As he came into the room in the wake of the others she looked at him eagerly, and he felt her eyes upon him, and grinned. For a moment her heart lifted; she felt the beginnings of a wild surge of relief. And then she realized that he wasn't really seeing her—not, anyway, as she wanted him to see her. He had smiled at her automatically, but his thoughts were somewhere quite different. In Rome, perhaps.

As the thought struck her for the first time, with all its implications, she swallowed, and Colonel Ryland, white-haired and benevolent, glanced at her sharply and told her that she looked tired. Silhouetted against the glowing aubergine of the curtains she looked very slight and fragile, an insubstantial figure in a slim dress of silver-grey shantung, and as they sat down Sue looked at her keenly too. She had been placed on the Colonel's left, which meant that the Conte di Lucca was on her other side, and John nowhere near her— an arrangement which normally would have disappointed her a little, but which at the moment she simply found rather a relief. She wanted nothing more than to be left alone, and as John and Alison Ryland, with able assistance from Sue and the Colonel, kept the conversation running almost incessantly she leant back a little in her chair, withdrawing herself from the others. She had no appetite, but as the skilfully prepared courses came and went before her she did her best to eat, recognizing that if she did so she would at least draw less attention to herself.

And after a time she began to realize that she wasn't the only person present who was inclined to be silent. The Conte di Lucca, she noticed, rarely spoke unless it was absolutely necessary. From time to time the others plied him with questions about Italy, and particularly about life in modern Rome, with which he seemed well acquainted, but for a good deal of the time he said nothing whatsoever, and glancing at him Candy got the impression, once or twice, that he wasn't really conscious of his surroundings. To her his detachment was so noticeable—though she didn't think anyone else around the dinner-table was aware of it—that despite her own dull bewilderment it caught her attention, and she found herself studying him surreptitiously. He seemed to be brooding on something, and as she watched him it struck her suddenly that when his face was in repose he looked like a man for whom life had become rather tasteless.

And then Sue said something funny, and he laughed with infectious boyish amusement, looking utterly transformed. Candy decided that her imagination had been running away with her, and as Mrs. Ryland led the move to the drawing-room she left the table with relief.

Outside the dining-room door Sue turned to her, looking anxious.

"Listen, Candy, are you all right? You hardly touched anything at dinner, and you look sort of—well. . . ." She paused. She knew quite well what was the matter with Candy, and she felt wretched about it, but she didn't know what to say—she didn't even know whether it would be wise to say anything, at this point. "I know it isn't just the audition," she ventured, clumsily feeling her way. "It isn't, is it?"

Candy bit her lip, fighting a childish urge to burst into tears on the spot. "I'll pour the coffee," she said, and abruptly she moved away. Later on she might have to talk to Sue about it—well, she'd have to say something, at least—but she didn't need to do it now.

Her fingers shook as she manipulated the heavy silver coffee-pot, but Sue took her cup without a word, and she knew that for the next hour or so she was safe. And then the men came in, and without looking up she poured more coffee.

And, almost before she realized it, John was standing over her.

"Hello, Candy." There was an uncertain smile on his lips—an odd smile.

"Hello, John." Her voice was admirably cool and natural, and the effort behind it didn't even show in her face. With a hand that she was fiercely willing to remain steady she held a cup out to him. "What was Rome like?"

"Rome was amazing. You'd like it." He sipped his coffee, and glanced down at her. "You'll go there some day. Everybody should."

With detachment, she reflected that since dinner his attitude to her seemed to have changed slightly. It was as if he had suddenly recollected her existence, and it troubled him.

"Did you get all the material you needed?" She asked the question automatically, and was grateful for the sudden arrival on her lap of Mrs. Ryland's Abyssinian cat. It gave her something to do with her hands, now that her coffee-pouring duties were temporarily fulfilled.

"Yes, I got pretty well everything. And if there are any gaps left di Lucca will fill them in." He glanced at the Italian, now seated beside Sue on the other side of the room. "The programme will deal with modern Roman society—high society, you might say—and I shouldn't think there's much he doesn't know about that particular subject. His following me over is a bit of luck, actually—I didn't know he was here until I ran into him in London the other day."

He had been back, then, for several days at least. That was obvious. He seemed to realize that he had betrayed the fact, and to feel vaguely uncomfortable about it, but he didn't attempt to explain why Candy hadn't known he was in England. He hadn't even said, so far, that he had missed her, but now that her mind was clearing a little that didn't surprise her—he obviously hadn't missed her. Something had happened in Rome that had changed things completely. She was going to have to adjust to the fact, that was all. She didn't yet know how she was going to adjust to it, but the effort had got to be made.

For something to say, she asked him whether he had met the Conte di Lucca in Rome, and for a moment she thought that he looked a little odd—that his embarrassment increased slightly.

"Yes . . . we were introduced by a—by a sort of contact of mine." He set his coffee cup down, and stroked the cat. "Listen, Candy—" he began.

And then Sue's voice interrupted them.

"Come over here, Candy. We're talking about you."

John turned away, and she slowly stood up and moved over to stand beside her sister. As she reached them, the Italian got to his feet.

"Darling," said Sue, with a swift, faintly apologetic smile, "I'm going to ask you to do something—or rather, the Conte is."

The Conte smiled at her too, and in a detached way she noticed that there was a good deal of charm and

27

sweetness about the smile. "I should not ask," he said. "You are perhaps tired."

Her bewilderment showed in her face, and he smiled again. "It is only," he said, "that I would so much like to hear you sing, *signorina*."

"Oh!" she said. Her face, which had been rather white, was suddenly suffused with delicate colour. "I—I couldn't sing *now*!'"

Sue glanced up at her. "Why ever not? After all, you were to have sung to-night. There's a piano over there, and the Conte says he'll accompany you."

"Oh, no!" Candy's colour deserted her, leaving her, if anything, paler than before. "I really couldn't—I mean," hastily, "there's nothing to hear." She looked at the Conte. "You'd be very disappointed—my voice isn't world-shattering, or anything. . . ."

"But it is a charming voice, your sister tells me. And you were to have sung for Signor Caspelli to-night."

Once again Candy became conscious of something stricken in the depths of the brown eyes, and she hesitated, feeling a little ashamed of her own abruptness. "I'm a coward," she explained simply. "I don't expect I should have been able to sing in front of Signor Caspelli when it came to the point."

"I don't think you are a coward, *signorina*."

"Go on, Candy—sing something." There was an undercurrent of meaning in her sister's voice; Sue undoubtedly thought she was behaving like a child.

"Sing what you would have sung for Caspelli," urged the Conte. "I should like so much to hear you." His gentle, courteous insistence was very difficult to resist. Candy capitulated.

"I was to have sung *Caro Nome,*" she told him, adding hesitantly : "You know . . . ?"

"Of course . . . *Rigoletto.*" He stood up, walking to the piano, then waited for her to join him. As she did so, his dark eyes smiled into hers in a way that gave her a strange courage. "Don't be nervous," he advised softly. "Remember, even if you sing badly—which I think you won't—it is not the end of the world. There are worse things in life even than making oneself look or sound foolish. I think you know that already."

For a moment his gaze held hers, and then he sat down, and his fingers moved over the keyboard, bringing Verdi to life. Almost without thinking, she looked around the room. Sue, of course, was watching her, Colonel and Mrs. Ryland were watching her—from a position near the fireplace, even John was casually watching her. Something seemed to tighten up inside her throat, and although she tried to sing she couldn't. Skilfully, the Italian covered up for her, but his eyes were reproachful—even, as she had thought earlier, faintly contemptuous—and his disapproval brought her to her senses. She began to sing, her clear, soft soprano ringing through the quiet room with such melodious purity that the man at the piano looked up at her rather quickly, and even John, bending to throw the last of his cigarette into the fire, glanced round in surprise. Her voice had a very youthful quality, but it had something else as well—the power to convey tremendous depth of feeling. As she made her way through the famous aria all the tragic pathos surrounding the ill-fated Gilda seemed to surround her, and possibly because she herself suddenly felt so lost and vulnerable

29

she almost accidentally managed to convey the vulnerability of Verdi's heroine so effectively that before she had finished Sue began to be aware of a prickling sensation in her throat, and even Colonel Ryland, himself no opera-lover, put his brandy aside and muttered to his wife that the girl was good.

When she had finished there was a spontaneous burst of applause, and three of the listeners urged her to sing again, but the Conte di Lucca sat quite still in front of the keyboard, and for at least thirty seconds said nothing at all. Then he stood up and bowed.

"Thank you, Miss Wells. You have a fine voice."

She looked at him a little vaguely, and he smiled, rather as he might have smiled at a clever child, and repeated what he had said.

"You have a very good voice. Take care of it."

"Tell her to sing something else, Conte." Sue, bursting with gratification, was beaming across at Candy.

"Not to-night. I think she is a little tired." His voice was firm, and Candy was grateful for the understanding behind the words. She felt flat, and drained of all energy, and the knowledge that she had just sung a difficult aria with more power and artistry than she had ever commanded in her life before meant very little to her. It was over, and that was the main thing. All she wanted now was to go to bed, and without much caring what anyone thought of her she abruptly said so. Sue opened her mouth to protest, but a glance from her mother-in-law checked her, and the Italian, having closed the piano, moved to open the door for her.

"Good-night, *signorina*."

"Good-night." She looked around the room, and quite without meaning to, caught John's eye. He looked away quickly, and she knew he was relieved because he wouldn't have to talk to her any more that night. A feeling of finality came over her; she supposed it was just a section of her life that had ended, but it felt more like the end of everything.

A chorus of slightly embarrassed 'good-nights' followed her out into the hall...and then the Conte firmly closed the door behind her, and she was alone. More alone than she had ever been in her life before.

The grandfather clock began to chime ten, and she shook her head as if to clear it of something, then moved slowly up the stairs to her room.

CHAPTER THREE

THE following day was Sunday, and in Great Mincham it was Harvest Festival. After breakfast Colonel and Mrs. Ryland, Sue and Candy went to church—what the Roman Catholic Conte di Lucca did wasn't clear, but Candy supposed he might have gone to Mass. It was a wonderful autumn morning, and as after the service they walked back to the house through a drifting carpet of yellow beech leaves the ache inside her seemed to ease a little, as if a soothing balm had been applied to it. For a while she walked between Sue and Colonel Ryland, and then, quite deliberately it seemed, John dropped back to join them, and Sue with elaborate tact walked on with the Colonel.

For a while they walked in silence, while Candy's heart began to thump a little, and then, abruptly, the man beside her spoke.

"Candy. . . ."

"Yes?" Her eyes were on the sky, tracking the flight of a solitary jackdaw, and she didn't look at him.

"That singing of yours last night—it was quite something. I . . ." He hesitated and laughed, rather uncomfortably. "I didn't know you had it in you."

"I haven't sung much lately—at least, not during the last year or so." If he was only going to make polite conversation, why did he have to talk to her at all? She added: "And I didn't really sing well last night.

Your friend is a very good pianist—his accompaniment helped a lot."

"Don't be absurd." He was obviously irritated. "You've got a real talent. You must know that. It's time something was done about it ... something concrete."

She said nothing.

"It's too bad you couldn't keep that appointment with Caspelli, but—well, there are other possibilities, you know. Good voices—really good voices—aren't all that common, and the big names in the operatic world are always on the look-out. For instance, when I was in Rome. . . ." He hesitated, and then went on rather quickly. "When I was in Rome I heard of a chap who has spent his life making that sort of 'discovery'. He searches them out, then trains them and does everything necessary to groom them for stardom, as it were. The rest is up to them, of course, and they don't all make it, but I know for a fact that quite a number of his ducklings have turned into swans."

Half listening to him, half swallowing back a ridiculous urge to burst into tears, Candy murmured something inaudible.

"What I'm getting at," he went on, not looking at her, but apparently determined not to be put off, "is that this particular chap does it all for nothing—as far as the pupil is concerned, anyway. He'd do it for you."

Scarcely hearing what he said, Candy repeated automatically : "Do it for me?"

"Of course he would. I'd say it's a certainty. All you

have to do is apply for an audition...he has representatives in places like London and Paris. You know— people who sift through the local talent and send the pick of it on to him."

"I don't want to be sent anywhere," she told him flatly.

"Now don't be absurd, my sweet. You want to do something with your life, don't you?"

He was looking acutely uncomfortable, she realized that now, and she sensed, too, that he very much wanted her to do what he suggested. She thought she knew why.

"Don't feel responsible for me, John." She was standing still, now, in the middle of the road. On either side of them quiet meadows and patches of golden stubble stretched to the misty skyline, and there was no sound anywhere but the slowly retreating footsteps of the Rylands and the song of a bullfinch perched in the hedge. In the clarity of the autumn light her hair glowed more vividly than the beech leaves, and her eyes, wide and troubled, were like reed-shadowed pools.

John put his hands in his pockets, and kicked at a pebble. "Of course I feel responsible for you—we've known one another a long time, haven't we?"

"Yes."

"Well.... Naturally I take an interest in you. I want to see you make use of your talents—get something out of them."

Strange, she thought abstractedly, that he had never before seemed to realize she had any talents. The same thought evidently occurred to him.

34

"I didn't know you could sing—I mean, not like that. Look—Candy, are you listening to me?"

As she looked at him her eyes were almost expressionless. "I'm listening, John."

"I want you to do as I say. Go to London and see this fellow's representative—have an audition. Before you know where you are you'll be in Rome, training for La Scala."

"I don't want to go to Rome," she told him. "I don't want to be a singer." Deep inside her, something seemed to add that just now she didn't want to be anything. Existence itself looked unbearably drab.

"But why not at least give it a try? If nothing else, it'd be an experience."

And it might salve your conscience, she thought wearily. Suddenly everything seemed clear. While he was in Rome, something—or someone—very important had happened to John, and now, because of it, he saw everything in life differently. In particular, he saw her, Candy, differently—or rather, perhaps, he hardly saw her at all, except as a being towards whom he felt a duty.

And all this meant that for her, too, life was different. So different that it hardly had any meaning left. Without John, she had no desires or ambitions, no hopes ... or even fears. In fact she found it difficult, suddenly, to imagine the future at all. By far the easiest thing, since she had no wishes of her own, would be to fall in with the suggestions of others. And since she loved John— since, even now, she felt the urge to do what would make him happier—she might as well, she supposed, fall

35

in with his suggestion. It *would* ease his conscience, that was obvious, and nothing else mattered very much.

She would go to London and have this audition, if it were possible. Sue would probably be pleased, too. She might be successful, and she might not. But beyond the audition nothing mattered anyway, because beyond the audition John would not be involved.

CHAPTER FOUR

THREE weeks later, flying over the Alps on a cold, brilliant day of early winter, Candy found herself wondering, suddenly, what she was doing. Until that moment she had not thought much about it, for most of the time lately she had lived in a kind of daze, out of contact, almost, with reality, and the significance of what was happening in her life had glanced off her. But now, all at once, realization came to her—and with it a slight feeling of dizziness, and a sinking sensation in her stomach which she hadn't even begun to feel when they were taking off.

She was on board an airliner bound for Rome, and with her, in the three or four items of her not very smart luggage, she was carrying almost everything she possesed in the world. For her stay in Italy was likely to be a lengthy one, and there had been no point in leaving any of her things behind in England . . . even if she had been able to find accommodation for them, which would have been difficult. Her tiny flat in Kensington had been given up, and there was only Sue— she didn't want to trouble Sue, who had put herself out quite enough already.

There had been so much to do, so much to arrange in the course of this last fortnight, that without her sister Candy didn't suppose she would possibly have been ready in time—not that that would have worried her very much, but it would, she knew, have worried Sue. The audition had been arranged so swiftly ... she had barely had time to think about it before she was summoned to present herself at a rendezvous in Kensington, where she was to be met by an Italian gentleman known as Signor Maruga. Apparently—so Sue discovered—Signor Maruga was quite a well-known personality in the world of music, and his connections in Italy were even better known. In Italian eyes, as far as Sue could gather, they even had the edge on Signor Caspelli.

Giacomo Maruga was short and plump, and he was gifted with a cherubic cheerfulness which Candy found oddly soothing. At the time of the audition she had had no nerves because, on the whole, it all meant very little to her, and yet at the same time she had done her best for Sue's sake. The result had been that she had sung as she had never sung before, and Signor Maruga, his dark eyes sparkling with approval, had taken her hand in his and assured her that his good friend Lorenzo Galleo would certainly be delighted to see her in Rome. Everything that Signor Galleo could do to train her voice and shape her career would, he promised, be done, and she would have no need to trouble about finance.

"A voice like yours, *signorina*," he had said, "is a gift from God—not only to you but to the whole world, if it is properly handled. It must be cherished, it must be brought to perfection—and that, *signorina*, you may safely leave to Lorenzo Galleo."

And so all the arrangements had been made—largely by Sue and Signor Maruga, who put their heads together and discussed things over Candy's head very much as if she were already a temperamental, impractical prima donna who must not on any account be worried with mundane trivialities. All of which was perfectly satisfactory as far as Candy was concerned, for she had no real interest in either the details or the main purpose of the adventure that lay ahead of her. She rather wished she didn't have to go to Rome, for it was in Rome that that mysterious something had happened to John that had taken him away from her, but on the whole it didn't seem to her to matter very much where she went. Wherever she went, there would be no John, and she knew now that for the last three years, although she had not quite realized it, he had been the central pivot of her life. For her, life had revolved around John, and without it was a meaningless jumble, coming from nowhere and going nowhere.

She had last seen him at Great Mincham, on the evening of the day when they had walked back from church together, and he had urged her to go ahead with her singing, and try for the patronage of Signor Galleo. She would remember that evening, she thought, as long as she lived—not because of anything that had happened, for very little had happened, but simply because of the tortures she had endured as the quiet hours of the rural Sunday slipped away, and she, surrounded by people but more alone than she had ever been in her life before, had struggled to come to terms with the upheaval going on in the depths of her mind and soul. Her sense of desolation had been so new, then, that she had not known whether she was going to be able to cope with it or not. The mists surrounding her had seemed so very dense, and she had not been able to see any way through them. Having satisfied his conscience by giving her the benefit of his advice John had said very little more to her, and when, that night, she went to bed early with a headache, they merely said good-night to one another. The next day when she went down to breakfast he was gone, and she hadn't seen him since.

So that chapter of her life was over, and another chapter, if one could call it that, had begun. But it wasn't like living, it was more like existing in a perpetual dream—an unclear, vaguely worrying dream in which all colour had been drained out of the world. Other people were alive and experiencing the full range of human emotions—happiness and misery, excitement and disappointment, boredom and exhilaration—but for the last three weeks Candy had had the peculiar feeling that she was not alive at all.

Until now. Now, with a mildly painful sensation like the coming to life of a limb that has 'gone to sleep', something stirred inside her, and the knowledge of what she was doing jabbed at her with the violence of a sharp needle. She was going away from everything she knew to a country she had never seen, and she was going to live among people whose whole culture, temperament and way of life were utterly strange to her. She hadn't met many Italians in the course of her life so far, and the only two she was able to remember with any clarity were Signor Maruga and the faintly mysterious figure of the Conte di Lucca, who had left the week-end party at Great Mincham early on Sunday afternoon. She had spoken to him very little, but before he left he had thanked her for having sung for him, and as she thought of him now his thoughtful dark eyes seemed to hover in front of her as vividly as if he had been sitting opposite her. There had still been pity in those eyes when they had last looked at her, but it had still been mildly contemptuous pity. The thought of the Conte di Lucca made Italy a little alarming, and she tried to shut those eyes out of her consciousness.

It was just getting dark as they began to circle Rome, and the Seven Hills were ablaze with light. Gazing down through the November dusk Candy could see very little, apart from the lights, but all at once it occurred to her that somewhere down there, only a few thousand feet below the throbbing shape of the aircraft, was spread a huge and famous city, one of the oldest and one of the most beautiful cities in the world, and just for a moment a twinge of something like excitement shot through her. But it was only a passing sensation, and the next instant all she knew was that she was feeling tired and a little panicky.

Smoothly and without any sort of hitch they landed, and she heard the voice of the stewardess instructing passengers to unfasten their seat-belts and prepare to leave the aircraft. The plane was not going on beyond Rome, and everyone on board had reached their destination. Feeling very stiff, she stood up and moved along the central aisle. Just in front of her a fatherly-looking Spaniard travelling alone with two small boys was rather anxiously telling his charges to comb their sleek black hair, and button up the jackets of their neat, dark brown, unchildish suits, and in front of him an attractive girl who was probably Italian was quite unmistakably

41

smiling to herself. She looked as if she were walking on air, and Candy wondered who it was she was expecting to meet at the airport. A fiancé, probably, she thought; or at any rate someone who stood a reasonable chance of becoming a fiancé within the foreseeable future. It must be wonderful, she thought, to be so completely happy at the thought of being with another human being. She had never known that feeling—not quite, although John.... She caught herself up sharply, annoyed with herself for having allowed her thoughts to stray into forbidden territory, and then the queue of disembarking passengers began to move forward more quickly, and the next moment she was at the head of the gangway, feeling the soft touch of warm rain on her face. The air was soft, too, and it seemed to caress her. As she moved down the steps and then set off across the tarmac she suddenly felt curiously soothed.

But the feeling didn't last for long. The airport was very large and very modern and in parts very attractive, but it was also very frightening—at least to Candy, who had never before been abroad for so much as a summer holiday. Everywhere there seemed to be signs giving instructions in every imaginable language but English—or it could, she was willing to admit, simply have been that her bewildered eyes just weren't capable of locating the English bits. Moving with the stream, however, she eventually found her way through Customs and Immigration, and then stood staring helplessly at the bustling tide of humanity flowing all around her. Even the eyes of the Customs officers had brightened with perceptible Latin appreciation at sight of her trim, insubstantial figure, and the way the warm gold of her light woollen suit complemented her eyes and her swinging hair, and now, standing unattended in the midst of the main reception hall, she found the strongly interested glances of dark-eyed passers-by acutely embarrassing.

She knew that someone was supposed to be meeting her, but nobody appeared to be looking out for her, and so far her name hadn't been mentioned on the public address system. Despite the mildness of the atmosphere she began to feel rather cold, and when more than ten minutes had elapsed and still there was no indication that anyone was giving her a thought something seemed to start turning over inside her. At last fifteen minutes were up, and almost all of those who had travelled from London with her had been absorbed into the mysterious world beyond the main doors of the airport. Some were collected by relatives and friends and borne away in sleek Italian cars; others departed by bus or taxi, but nobody apart from Candy seemed in any way lost. The anxious-looking man with the two small boys was reunited with a plump and beaming matron who could only have been the children's mother, and after hugging one another more or less incessantly for about five minutes the whole party went off happily in a battered Volkswagen. Candy even saw the Italian girl meet the man of whom she had obviously been thinking all the way from London. He was tall and good-looking and they made an attractive pair. She watched them as they stood gazing at one another in the midst of the hurrying crowds, and she watched them as they finally disappeared from sight through the swing doors of the airport . . . but then, just as another cold wave of misery was about to break over her, she remembered where she was and what she was doing, and the thought of John was pushed out of her head by the thought of her present position.

She fumbled in her handbag for the address of the place that was to be her home for the next few months ... the Convent of the Holy Angels, Via Santa Cristina, Rome. If she wasn't going to be met there was no doubt about it—she'd better take a taxi. A bus, of course, would be very much cheaper, but it would also be something of an ordeal. She didn't know how to set about finding the right one, and then there were all those staring eyes.... Whatever the taxi cost her, it would be worth it.

She moved outside, struggling not to look over-burdened by the three suitcases she was trying to man-age single-handed, and soon managed to attract the attention of a taxi-driver. He was middle-aged and paternal, and although he obviously considered her well worth looking at he didn't have the effect of making her feel uncomfortable. She showed him the address of the convent, and he nodded and took all her cases from her simultaneously.

"*Si, signorina.* You get in and not worry, uh?"

With a sigh of relief she obeyed, sinking back on to the comfortable rear seat of the taxi, and as the curious eyes and the airport lights swirled away from her and they plunged into the mainstream of traffic heading towards Rome it sank into her consciousness at last that she was actually in Italy. It was an Italy of which she couldn't yet see very much, despite the brilliance of the street lighting, for most of the time they seemed to be somewhere in the middle of a vast river of rushing traffic, but there was a strangeness in the air that touched her with a hint of excitement which she hadn't expected to feel, and the faces in the cars moving on either side of the long gleaming taxi were strange too— strange, but vividly interesting. Some of the faces, she noticed, were strikingly attractive, with the chiselled features of ancient Rome and the black hair and eyes of the South, and the women tended to have lovely, flawless skin and a look of having been dressed by the top couturiers. Tired as she was, the faces fascinated her, and they kept her attention occupied for a long time. And then, all at once, they were drawing near to the heart of Rome, and the roads became slightly narrower. She saw great buildings that looked like palaces, glorious archways and shadowy ruins that in the past had looked at her a hundred times from photographs. In all directions the strong white light of the street lamps threw into vivid prominence the figures of Popes and Apostles, poets and emperors, saints and princes whose names had become interwoven with the life and breath of Rome, and every so often they flashed through a lovely piazza where fountains played and a few flower-sellers still lingered until late in the autumn evening to tempt the passers-by.

The size and beauty and splendour of everything around her overwhelmed Candy, and her own insignificance struck her rather violently. She began to be conscious of feeling tired and a little lost, and despite the breathtaking wonder outside the windows of the taxi she knew she would be glad when her destination was reached. Rome would still be there in the morning, and perhaps then she would feel more like taking it in —perhaps then it wouldn't seem so frightening.

All the arrangements for her stay in Rome had been undertaken for her by the assistants of Signor Maruga, and they had decided that at least until she had had time to find her feet in their capital city she should be accommodated in the guest house of a Benedictine convent which was situated, she understood, not far from the magnificent bulk of St. Peter's itself. She had never before stayed in a convent, and the idea had seemed strange when it was first mentioned to her, but now it struck her that in the midst of this sea of noise and bustle and confusing, conflicting impressions the tranquillity of the cloister would be a very pleasant refuge.

They entered a maze of narrow streets and tiny squares, and the noise of the trffic died away, to be replaced by the rushing of fountains and the shouts of small tousle-haired *raggazzi* who ought to have been in bed. At the street corners lights burned beneath brightly coloured images of the Virgin and the saints, and every now and then, from an upper window, there was a burst of music. Even inside the taxi Candy could hear it. One moment it was a radio, blaring forth the latest money-spinner from the world of Italian pop, the next it was a wonderful cascade of Beethoven from an unseen piano. She was fascinated, and absorbed in the sights and sounds of the streets she didn't realize they had reached their destination until the taxi-driver got out to open the door for her.

Then she saw that they had come to a halt in the shadow of a very old wall. Set in the wall was a handsome iron-studded door, and over the door a swinging

46

lantern shed light upon a small, gleaming brass plaque to one side of it.

"The Convent of the Holy Angels," said the taxi-driver in careful English, and extricated Candy's suit-cases from the boot. He stuffed all three cases more or less under one arm, and with his free hand pulled the bell-chain that hung beside the stout old door. Candy got out of his taxi and stood beside him, and as she stared up at the finely carved iron-work of the lantern he thought she looked very white.

"You are tired, *signorina*? You make a long journey to-day?"

She smiled and shook her head, so that her uncovered hair swung around her.

"It was a long journey, but a very easy one."

"Yet you are tired. Now that you are in Rome you will rest."

She was just about to disabuse him of any idea that she had come to Rome to rest when a light suddenly appeared behind a tiny window next to the doorway in front of them, and she saw that a nun was looking out.

"The Sisters wish to know who you are," the taxi-driver told her. "It is their custom. It is very old. They cannot open the door until they know who you are." He bent towards the beautiful, finely wrought grille that protected the window and said something in extremely rapid Italian. The nun seemed to hesitate, and she bent her head a little to study the English girl more closely through the thin, ornate bars that separated them.

"You say that we are expecting, you, *signorina*?" Her voice was quiet and soft, and her English very good.

"Yes." Candy moved closer to the tiny aperture, feeling very much as if she had suddenly stepped back into the Middle Ages. "Well, I ... I think so. Signor Maruga made all the arrangements."

"Signor Maruga ... ?" It could hardly have been called a frown, but a faint pucker certainly did appear between the nun's slim, straight brows. Then she smiled.

"Wait, I will let you in. Then you can explain to us."

She disappeared, and Candy swallowed and glanced at the patient taxi-driver.

Two minutes later the doors in front of them swung open, and another nun appeared. Once again the taxi-driver spoke quickly, and she nodded and smiled, and told him to leave the suitcases just inside the door. Then she beckoned Candy inside, and when she had paid the driver he touched his cap and beamed on her paternally.

"You will be all right now," he told her. "With the Sisters you will be all right."

Candy stepped across the worn threshold of the Convent, and as the outer door closed she glanced uncertainly at the white-robed figure beside her.

"*Is* it all right?" she asked, a little anxiously. "Can I stay here?"

The Sister smiled with the tranquillity of a being for whom no problem is insoluble.

"I am sure you can stay, *signorina*. Come with me."

They passed through into a small cloistered court-yard, where three more dim lanterns shone on the exquisite tracery above rows of Renaissance arches, and a tiny fountain gushed softly in the stillness of the evening. And in the shadows on the far side of the

48

lantern shed light upon a small, gleaming brass plaque to one side of it.

"The Convent of the Holy Angels," said the taxi-driver in careful English, and extricated Candy's suit-cases from the boot. He stuffed all three cases more or less under one arm, and with his free hand pulled the bell-chain that hung beside the stout old door. Candy got out of his taxi and stood beside him, and as she stared up at the finely carved iron-work of the lantern he thought she looked very white.

"You are tired, *signorina*? You make a long journey to-day?"

She smiled and shook her head, so that her uncovered hair swung around her.

"It was a long journey, but a very easy one."

"Yet you are tired. Now that you are in Rome you will rest."

She was just about to disabuse him of any idea that she had come to Rome to rest when a light suddenly appeared behind a tiny window next to the doorway in front of them, and she saw that a nun was looking out.

"The Sisters wish to know who you are," the taxi-driver told her. "It is their custom. It is very old. They cannot open the door until they know who you are." He bent towards the beautiful, finely wrought grille that protected the window and said something in ex-tremely rapid Italian. The nun seemed to hesitate, and she bent her head a little to study the English girl more closely through the thin, ornate bars that separated them.

"You say that we are expecting, you, *signorina*?" Her voice was quiet and soft, and her English very good.

"Yes." Candy moved closer to the tiny aperture, feeling very much as if she had suddenly stepped back into the Middle Ages. "Well, I . . . I think so. Signor Maruga made all the arrangements."

"Signor Maruga . . . ?" It could hardly have been called a frown, but a faint pucker certainly did appear between the nun's slim, straight brows. Then she smiled.

"Wait, I will let you in. Then you can explain to us."

She disappeared, and Candy swallowed and glanced at the patient taxi-driver.

Two minutes later the doors in front of them swung open, and another nun appeared. Once again the taxi-driver spoke quickly, and she nodded and smiled, and told him to leave the suitcases just inside the door. Then she beckoned Candy inside, and when she had paid the driver he touched his cap and beamed on her paternally.

"You will be all right now," he told her. "With the Sisters you will be all right."

Candy stepped across the worn threshold of the Convent, and as the outer door closed she glanced uncertainly at the white-robed figure beside her.

"*Is* it all right?" she asked, a little anxiously. "Can I stay here?"

The Sister smiled with the tranquillity of a being for whom no problem is insoluble.

"I am sure you can stay, *signorina*. Come with me."

They passed through into a small cloistered courtyard, where three more dim lanterns shone on the exquisite tracery above rows of Renaissance arches, and a tiny fountain gushed softly in the stillness of the evening. And in the shadows on the far side of the

48

courtyard the nun escorting Candy came to a halt beside a narrow door. She knocked, and then almost immediately turned the handle and gestured to Candy to go in ahead of her.

The English girl found herself in a small, square, white-walled room, very plainly and sparsely furnished. Against the wall there stood a black oak bookcase filled with books and a prie-dieu with a simple crucifix above it, and in the middle of the room, under the central light, there was an enormous and very tidy deal desk. Two women were sitting facing one another across the desk—one a nun in immaculate white, the other a slim, black-haired girl in the dress of fashionable modern Rome.

The nun who had accompanied Candy said something quietly, and her fellow behind the desk looked up and smiled.

"Ah! We are expecting you, *signorina*. What is your name?"

Candy told her, and her expression changed.

"You are Candida Wells?"

"Yes."

The nun's rather humorous mouth curved into a wry smile, and she looked across at the young woman sitting opposite her.

"What a coincidence!" she remarked in English. "But there has been a mistake, I think. We were not expecting you until to-morrow, Signorina Wells. It was to-morrow, was it not?" And she looked again at her companion from the outside world, who had risen to her feet, and was studying Candy with interest.

"Yes, Sister, I thought it was to-morrow. But this

49

must be my fault." The young woman's voice was as soft and gentle as the voices of the nuns, and she had the same air of detachment from the rough-and-tumble of the world, but when she turned round Candy realized that she wasn't quite as young as she had seemed at first. There was something about her that at first glance gave an impression of extreme youth, but a closer look at her serious dark eyes and neat features told Candy that she was probably about thirty. She made a small, very Latin gesture with one well-manicured hand, and smiled apologetically.

"I thought you would be here on the ninth, but it must have been the eighth. I often make such mistakes. I am very sorry."

She looked intensely worried, and Candy, already tired and bewildered, felt uncomfortable as well. The nun behind the desk intervened.

"Signorina Marchetti arranged for you to stay with us, Miss Wells, but unfortunately there seems to have been a little confusion. We were not expecting you until to-morrow, but, as you say in England, no harm has been done." She smiled reassuringly at Candy. "Our guest-house is really full, but we shall accommodate you." She didn't look worried, but Candy had a feeling that she might have added 'somehow'. Signorina Marchetti leant towards her across the desk, and said something quietly and urgently. The two women talked in Italian for about a minute, and then the nun spoke to Candy again.

"The Signorina suggests that you stay with her to-night. She has a most charming flat not far from here, and with her"—she shrugged and smiled—"you

will be much more comfortable than you would be in our guest-house. But you must tell me what you would like to do."

Candy felt more bewildered than ever. Although they were careful not to betray the fact, it was obvious that if she stayed with the nuns she would definitely be putting them to some sort of inconvenience. But on the other hand it seemed a bit much that this strange Italian woman should be expected to entertain her— even though she was, presumably, some sort of agent of Signor Maruga.

"It's very kind of you. . . ." She looked at Signorina Marchetti, and hesitated. "If you're sure it's not too much trouble?"

"To me it is no trouble." The other woman spoke almost eagerly. "I shall be most happy if you will agree to stay with me—for to-night at least. Your trunks . . . they are here?"

Candy nodded a little wryly, thinking of her three small cases reposing in the outer porch of the convent. "Yes, my luggage is here. But there isn't very much of it."

"Then we will go. In the morning, if you wish, you may return here."

The nuns smiled at Candy, and 'arrivedercis' were exchanged in all directions. Robed figures escorted the two young women from the outer world back across the little courtyard and through the echoing passageway to the massive main door leading on to the street. Outside, in the late evening tranquillity of the Via Santa Cristina, Signorina Marchetti's car was waiting, drawn up rather quaintly on the pavement, and before the

English girl knew quite what was happening one of the nuns had briskly seized her suitcases and deposited them in the Signorina's boot. Then, smiling at her distressed expression, they opened the car door for her and helped her inside. She noticed that before stepping back one of them stroked the gleaming paintwork of the vehicle with a kind of childlike pleasure.

The car, a streamlined Italian model which would have cost a fortune in England and probably hadn't cost so very much less in Rome, moved off with nothing more than a subdued purring sound, and as it slid quietly down the narrow street and round the corner into a piazza the woman behind the wheel glanced at Candy.

"We have not been introduced," she remarked. "I am Caterina Marchetti. I was asked to make the arrangements for your stay in Rome, and to"—her serious mouth relaxed a little into a half smile—"and to 'keep an eye' on you ... that is the term, I think."

"It's very good of you," said Candy, feeling slightly awkward. "I'm afraid I'm causing rather a lot of trouble."

The Signorina shook her head. "For me it is no trouble."

They came to a halt in a quiet cul-de-sac, outside a high stone building where one or two lights still gleamed behind heavy curtains, and where a general air of expensive sobriety indicated to Candy that they had reached a rather exclusive corner of the city. Signorina Marchetti got out of the car and beckoned what was evidently a porter from the shadows of the doorway before which they had come to rest, and the English girl followed her out on to the pavement just in time to see her suitcases being borne through swinging glass doors into the entrance hall of what seemed to be quite a luxurious block of flats.

The hall, when they went in, was large and rather dim, for it was lit only by a single lamp, which had been placed near the door, but as soon as she crossed the threshold Candy could see that she was in what must once have been one of the great *palazzi*, now converted into flats. In front of her a wide, shining marble staircase rose in a graceful curve towards the faintly visible splendours of a distant painted ceiling, and at the foot of the stairs the dully gleaming figures of bronze nymphs held aloft candelabra in which the last candles had long since been extinguished.

Signorina Marchetti hurried her guest past the antique glories of the staircase towards a corner where an ultra-modern lift had been installed, and together they ascended to the fourth floor, where the Signorina's own flat was located.

And, tired and dazed as she was, when she entered Signorina Marchetti's wide *salotto* Candy could only stand and gaze around her.

It was a room that had probably once been a bed-chamber—not one of the best bedchambers, for they would have been found on the lower floors, but still an apartment fit for a respected guest. Because it had never been one of the most important rooms its ceiling was not too uncomfortably high, and all in all, for a room in an ancient *palazzo* it had an astonishing air of cosiness about it. And at the same time it was bright and elegant, with white walls and tall windows, hidden at the moment behind curtains of gold brocade. There was a gold carpet that spread into every corner of the room, and the furniture was a subtle blend of twentieth-century comfort and Renaissance elegance.

Her hostess was talking to the porter, and almost too tired to move, Candy simply went on staring.

And then a figure suddenly rose from one of the massive, comfortable-looking armchairs, and she heard a man's voice speaking to her. Or at least, not to her, but to the person the speaker thought she was. The voice spoke Italian, and although she recognized it for a moment or two she couldn't think who it belonged to. And then the figure loomed up in front of her, and she blinked in astonishment.

For it was the Conti di Lucca who stood in front of her—a Conte di Lucca who looked as if the last week or two had done little or nothing for his spirits, and whose lean, tanned face looked rather haggard.

He was obviously very nearly as surprised as she was, but he was the first to recover.

"For a moment I thought I was dreaming," he said, staring at her. "But I was not asleep."

Then Signorina Marchetti appeared behind them, and she spoke quickly, almost agitatedly, in English.

"Michele! I did not know you would be here—you should have told me. . . ." She looked from the man to the drooping figure of the slim young Englishwoman, and it seemed to Candy, half asleep as she was, that Caterina Marchetti was taking in the fact that the other two knew each other, and not particularly liking it.

Presumably Michele di Lucca was either her fiancé

or something very similar, and the idea of his being on speaking terms with any other woman was a thing her Latin spirit resented fiercely just now.

All at once Candy thought of John, and how wonderful it would have been if he had been meeting her in Rome. Tears pricked behind her eyelids and she felt unutterably weary—too weary even to feel amazement at the extraordinary fact that within two hours of arriving in Italy she had run into the Conte di Lucca.

CHAPTER FIVE

THE following morning a neat little Italian maid
brought Candy her breakfast in bed, and as her bedroom
curtains were drawn back to admit the winter sunlight
and she struggled into wakefulness she realized that she
had overslept. It was after nine o'clock, and she had
intended to be up by seven. But when she asked the
maid to apologize for her to Signorina Marchetti the
girl only laughed, showing in the process two rows of
astonishingly pearly teeth.

"The Signorina's guests always have the breakfast
in bed," she explained, still smiling, and surveying
Candy with frank, uninhibited interest. "The Signorina,
she is always up early, but she likes that the guests be
comfortable. And also, you have long journey yesterday. She tell me not to wake you till now."

When the door had closed behind the maid Candy
moved her breakfast tray on to the bedside table and
slipped out of bed to look out of the window. At first
glance there was nothing to see but a narrow street
lined by tall, sombrely impressive stone buildings, but
after a moment or two she noticed that just opposite
her window there was a gap between two of the buildings, and the gap was filled by what was obviously a
garden wall. Over the top of the wall it was possible to
glimpse the upper branches of a tree . . . a fruit tree.
She thought at first that it was an apple tree, carrying

56

a burden of rather late and very golden apples—but then she remembered where she was, and when she looked again she saw that it was not apples but ripe lemons that were hanging in clusters on the other side of the wall. This was Rome, and there was a lemon-tree across the road.

Feeling suddenly unaccountably cheerful, she walked back to the bed and consumed a hearty breakfast of coffee, warm rolls and preserve.

Afterwards she dressed rather slowly, thinking about the previous evening. The Conti di Lucca had departed almost immediately, saying very little either to her or to their mutual hostess, and at the time she had been too tired to think very much about the coincidence of his being there. But the more she thought about it, the more extraordinary it seemed that the man she had met three weeks ago in Berkshire should, of all the men in Italy, turn out to be a close friend of the woman who had apparently been deputed by either Signor Maruga or Signor Calleo to take charge of her interests while she was in Rome. And perhaps the most amazing aspect was the fact that he himself had seemed to think so little of it.

As she slipped into a grey wool dress and brushed her hair until it shone she found herself wondering just how close the relationship between the Conte and Caterina Marchetti was. It was nothing, of course, to do with her, but there was something about Michele di Lucca that interested her—something that could have been described as tragic. She almost felt sorry for him, and yet somehow he wasn't the sort of man one pitied. It was difficult to say what sort of man he was, for although she didn't know much about him she was reasonably certain she had never met anyone like him before.

Outside her bedroom door she ran into her hostess, who had just come up in the lift and was now engaged in issuing instructions to her maid. She was wearing a smart cream-coloured jersey suit, and on her smooth dark head not a hair was out of place. It struck Candy, as it had done the night before, that the Italian woman was extremely good-looking, and possibly would have been more so if her hairstyle had been a little less severe and she had gone in for a little more make-up, and it occurred to her to wonder why Caterina Marchetti wasn't married.

Perhaps, she thought, the Conte di Lucca was in no great hurry to settle down.

At sight of Candy the Signorina smiled, and with effortless fluency switched instantaneously from rapid Italian to precise English.

"Good morning! You slept well? I hope Paolina did not awaken you too early."

Candy shook her head. "I'm afraid I overslept dreadfully."

"Nonsense. It was not late, even now, and you were so very tired. Come into the *salotto*, and we will talk."

As she spoke she pushed a door open, and together they went into the golden room that had enchanted Candy the night before. This morning one or two rays of pale sunshine were slanting through the windows on to the vivid carpet, and in the daylight the loveliness of the old gilded furniture showed up more clearly.

In the fireplace a small log fire was blazing, and

Signorina Marchetti suggested that they should sit beside it.

"Even in Rome it is cold in November," she remarked, "and to-day something has happened to the central heating. You are warm enough?"

Candy, who actually found the atmosphere a little stifling, assured her that she was quite warm enough. And then, because it was worrying her a little, she asked what she should do about getting in touch with the Convent of the Holy Angels.

"If I could telephone. . . ." she began.

"You wish to speak to them?" Caterina Marchetti looked rather perplexed. "But it is not necessary. I have arranged everything with them."

"Oh. . . . Then they are expecting me?"

"Expecting you? But of course not. I told them that while you are in Rome you will remain with me. It is a so much better arrangement." Her expression altered, and her dark eyes became puzzled and anxious. "You do not like it so? You would like better to go to the Convent?"

"But. . . ." Candy felt acutely embarrassed. "That's not the point. I can't possibly impose on you—I may be here for months."

"Please—you do not impose on me." The Italian woman's slender, expressive hands were spread a little dramatically. "I live all alone here, and for me it will be most pleasant. The idea did not come to me until last night, when the Sisters were unable to receive you, but now I see that nothing could be better." She added a litle dryly: "The Sisters *were* unable to receive you last night—if you had wanted to stay they would have

59

given up one of their own beds to you, but really they had no room."

"But. . . ." Candy began again, and stopped.

"Of course if you do not wish to stay with me I will telephone Sister Maria Giuseppina and tell her that I was wrong." The soft voice sounded hurt, and Candy saw that there was only one thing she could possibly do.

"I'd love to stay with you," she told the other woman warmly. "But if you get tired of having me—well, you must let me know."

"I shall not get tired," said Caterina Marchetti with confidence.

It had been arranged that Candy should have her first interview with Signor Galleo on the following day, so that afternoon she was free to do what she liked, and her hostess, who also seemed to have plenty of time on her hands, suggested that they should go out for a walk around Rome.

"We will not go to-day to see the great churches or the ancient ruins," she said. "You will have so much time for that. I am always sorry for the tourists who hurry from St. Peter's to the Colosseum, and then just stop to see quickly the Catacombs before driving on to Naples. They never see the soul of Rome. And then too much beauty and history at one time is hard to digest—like too much chocolate, yes?"

Candy enjoyed that afternoon as she could not remember enjoying anything for quite a long time. She and Caterina strolled at a leisurely pace through streets and squares that she had merely glimpsed the night before, and as they walked the Italian woman talked about their surroundings with the affectionate familiarity that came from having lived almost all her life in Rome. Long before they got to the end of their excursion Candy understood what she had meant about seeing the 'soul' of the city. The soul of Rome, she decided, was in its old yellow stones, in its quiet corners where broods of cats assembled around lovely, unexpected iron gateways and where little fountains played unseen by any but the most adventurous of the tourists. It was in the hundreds of colourful little shrines established by the faithful at street corners, and perhaps above all it was in the faces of old, work-weary women and in the shrieks of little boys playing Red Indians in the dark, narrow tunnels of the ancient *strade*. It was even, she thought, in the roar of the motor-scooters, the modern Roman's favourite means of transport. But however it was that she had discovered it, by the time she got back to Caterina Marchetti's apartment that day Candy really felt that she had glimpsed the essential spirit of the Eternal City.

That night, Caterina explained apologetically, she had to go out—and it was apparently not the sort of expedition on which she could invite her English guest to join her. If anything, Candy was relieved to know that she was to be left to herself for the evening, for she was tired and wanted to go to bed early, but she couldn't resist a touch of curiosity as to who it was who would be engaging her hostess's attention. Was it the Conte di Lucca, and if so *was* there some close relationship between them?

But Signorina Marchetti wasn't communicative on the

subject and if anybody did come to collect her Candy didn't see who it was. She herself had a light supper in her room—for she had firmly refused the formal meal in the dining-room that the Italian woman had wanted to insist she had—and very shortly afterwards she went to bed.

She awoke in the morning to the sound of torrential rain—rain that dropped from the heavens, as only Italian rain can, with a solid, drenching violence that struck her as being very nearly as alarming as a bad thunderstorm—and at the same moment she remembered that to-day she had to see Signor Galleo. The thought oppressed her, and the oppression grew as she toyed with her coffee and rolls, once again brought to her by Paolina on a tray. Deep down inside her the conviction was growing that there was something almost fraudulent about her being here in Rome. In all sincerity and without, she thought, being unduly modest, she didn't believe she had a great singing voice. In her own private opinion, in fact, her voice was no more than passable, and apart from that, the idea that she might become a professional soprano struck her as almost absurd. The idea had never entered her head until Sue, feeling that something ought to be done about her only sister, had decided that she might stand a chance of attracting the great Caspelli's attention, and then, helped by the daze of misery she had been in over John, the whole thing had snowballed until now here she was in a foreign country, accepting a lot of gratuitous help from a variety of people who were absolutely nothing to her. It was only since her arrival in Italy that she had been thinking clearly enough to see all this, but now, suddenly, the realities of the situation had come home to her, and they struck her as so absolutely awful that she pushed her breakfast away almost untouched, and for a good five minutes simply sat staring in front of her. It was rather a strenuous five minutes, for while the pretty antique clock on the writing-desk in her room was ticking away the seconds she was struggling to come to a decision about the whole course of her future life, and when the time was up she had made that decision.

For a moment or two she had been on the point of backing out—of giving up the whole thing, making apologetic explanations and returning to London on the first available plane. It was unquestionably the easy way out, and even taking into consideration the fascinations of Rome, it was tempting. But the empty vacuum that her life would become once she was safely back in London made her shiver a little. The years she had spent in London, she realized now, had been utterly aimless. They hadn't seemed so at the time—or if they had the aimlessness had been very pleasant—because John had been there to give them colour. But if there was one thing that seemed absolutely certain it was the fact that a future in which John didn't feature was something with which she had got to come to grips. The meaning had been taken out of her life, and a new meaning had to be found for it. Perhaps, here in Rome, that meaning would become clear. Signor Maruga and a number of other people had confidence in her, and their confidence was a challenge. She could at least try. . . .

She felt as if she were setting off blindfold along an arduous and lonely road, but once her decision had been reached her mind was clear, and when she stood up to comb her hair and get ready for her first interview with Signor Galleo she felt happier than she had done for weeks.

CHAPTER SIX

LORENZO GALLEO was a small man—at least, he wasn't tall—and at first sight Candy thought he looked rather insignificant. But that was before she had had time to notice the magnetism in his brilliant dark eyes, and to feel the full effects of his boundless, dynamic energy. After half an hour in his company she felt very much as if she had been caught up with a hurricane, and the experience had left her decidedly shaken. He said at once that he was anxious to hear her sing, and she was hardly given time even to decide whether she was nervous or not before her coat and gloves were whisked away from her, and his accompanist was leading the way into her favourite *Caro Nome*.

She sang well, she knew, though she couldn't imagine why; and when she had finished the maestro's gratification was obvious. He was silent for several seconds, and then he came over to her and squeezed her hands.

"My friend Giacome Maruga did not lie to me," he remarked. "You have a talent, *signorina*. Just now it is only a little talent—a very little, a tiny talent! But if you will work hard, and give your heart to your work, it will grow.... Let me look at you, please." He stood back, studying her critically. "For a *cantante*, you are very small and slim. And you look not strong. Are you strong enough for such a life?"

"I'm very healthy," she told him quietly. "I'm quite strong enough."

"*Bene, bene.* Then to-morrow we will begin to work." But something in her face still seemed to trouble him, and when his accompanist had been dismissed he passed a hand thoughtfully over his thinning black hair and gave her another very penetrating look. "You know, of course, the story of the opera *La Traviata.*"

"Yes, of course."

"As you know, it is a love-story—a sad and a dramatic story. When you take the part of Violetta you must put everything you have into your voice, for unless the audience are made to feel the power and the tragedy of her love your performance will be empty." He paused for breath, spreading his hands in an extravagant gesture. "When you are on the stage you must always remember that it is not you who are singing, but that other woman—the woman you are representing. Your music is very important—it is almost everything— but your music will be dead unless you realize this. You must try very hard to understand and to live everything that woman is supposed to be feeling. Joy, misery, anger, relief, boredom, contentment . . . love. Love, perhaps, is the most important of all. But. . . ." For a moment he paused again, allowing his square-tipped brown fingers to drum a little on the top of the piano. "But in your own life, *signorina*, for the moment at least, there must be no thought of love. As I told you, all your heart must be in your singing. You have been unhappy, one can see, but that is almost over, I think. Lose yourself in your music, Signorina Wells, forget everything else—

for a time, if not for ever. A brilliant artist cannot be an ordinary human being, remember that."

She said nothing, and he walked over to one of the wide windows, beckoning to her to follow him. The windows commanded a panoramic view of the city—a view so staggering that she caught her breath a little when she saw it.

"Rome is a great city, *no e vero*? One day, if you work hard—if you work very hard—it may be that you will become the fine singer I think you could be, and then . . . and then perhaps all that great city down there will be at your feet. And not only that city, but many others also, around Italy and around the world."

Candy followed the direction of his eyes. "I want to work," she told him. "Not because I think I might become famous"—she smiled rather enchantingly, causing him to relax and smile back—"but just because. . . ." Her voice trailed away, and she finished abruptly: "I want to work more than anything else in the world."

When she emerged from the elegant dimness of Signor Galleo's audition room she blinked a little in the unexpected brilliance of the winter sunlight, and it occurred to her that before she did anything else she was going to have to buy herself a pair of sunglasses. For a minute or two she stood hesitating on the well-scrubbed doorstep, wondering in which direction to start walking—for a taxi had delivered her to Signor Galleo's door, and Caterina Marchetti wasn't with her—and then, as she stood there, a man's voice suddenly spoke her name, and she jumped.

"*Mi dispiace* . . . I'm very sorry." The owner of the voice stood before her on the pavement, and she saw

that it was the Conte di Lucca. He had just emerged
from an expensive-looking low-slung white Fiat which
was parked beside the kerb, and in his beautifully cut
light grey suit and immaculate shirt, his dark hair
gleaming in the sun, he looked the most perfect example
anyone would be likely to meet of a well-dressed and
startlingly good-looking modern Italian nobleman.
Candy hadn't realized before that he was so good-
looking, and briefly and in a detached sort of way she
wondered why.

"I am sorry," he said again. "I startled you. Caterina
asked me to meet you, in case you should become lost
. . . but perhaps you would prefer not to be met?"

She smiled at him, crinkling her eyes a little against
the glare. "Thank you—it's very nice of you to take so
much trouble. But I don't want to be a burden to anyone. I can easily wander around by myself for a while,
and then just take a bus or a taxi back to Miss
Marchetti's flat."

He hesitated, looking for a moment as if, having
salved his conscience by making his offer of assistance,
he were now going to remove himself and let her do
exactly as she suggested. And then he shook his head.
"In Rome it's too easy to be lost. Tell me where you
wish to go and I will take you there."

"Oh, but I couldn't do that," she protested rather
vaguely. She would have liked to wander off by herself,
for she was feeling tense and suddenly exhausted after
the morning's ordeal, and she thought that finding her
way alone through the sunlit, crowded streets would
have been curiously relaxing. "I want to buy some sun-

glasses," she added, as if this admission might induce him to give her her freedom.

"Then first I will take you to a *farmacia*, and you may select a pair." He was holding the car door open for her, and she had no option but to climb inside.

They drew smoothly out into the mid-morning traffic, and reacting to the gentle warmth of the sun on her face, and the superlative comfort of the Fiat, Candy gradually began to feel more relaxed. After about five minutes they came to an excellent chemist's shop, where a smiling Italian girl helped her choose a pair of sunglasses from a range so varied and bewildering that by the time she emerged into the street again she was feeling almost dizzy, and the glasses she had chosen suited her so well that no fewer than four members of the male sex turned to give her an interested second look as she made her way from the shop doorway to the car.

But her escort hadn't entered the shop with her, and by the time she rejoined him he had got back into the driving-seat and was staring broodingly through the windscreen. He got out with courteous alacrity to open the car door for her, but he made no comment on the newly acquired sunglasses, and his sudden air of abstraction made her feel uncomfortable. She decided he must all at once have recollected some sort of engagement which made being burdened with her rather tiresome, and she quickly apologized for keeping him waiting outside the shop.

"If you haven't got time to drive me back to Miss Marchetti's flat I could still do what I intended to do," she assured him. "If you drop me here—"

He looked at her. "I have all the time in the world, *signorina*." And then after a moment he added : "Well, if not quite that, at least I can offer you to-day." The car increased speed a little, and he looked at his watch. "Do you take pleasure in hot chocolate?"

She was a little amused by his way of phrasing the question, but she answered : "Yes. Very much."

"Then I will take you to a café where one may see the whole of Rome pass by, and there you will taste chocolate which is worthy of the name."

For another two or three minutes they wound their way through the crowded, sunlit streets, and then the Conte found a suitable parking space, and when he had manoeuvred his sleek white car into it they both got out, and he guided her across the busy street to a place where, despite the fact that it was November, a few white-painted tables were already being arranged on the wide pavement. The café proprietor obviously knew the Conte well, and as they sat down amid the cheerful morning bustle of Rome he pulled their chairs out for them himself. He also looked at Candy as if she were quite the most delightful thing he had seen for months, and she was relieved when he disappeared to attend to the hot chocolate.

"I've never seen a pavement café before—not a real one, I mean," she told the Italian beside her. He had put on dark glasses himself now, which made him seem more detached than ever, and when she spoke he glanced at her abruptly, as if he had temporarily forgotten all about her.

"No?" he murmured. Politely, he added : "Do you like it?"

"Yes. But it's rather a strange sensation . . . sitting here, almost in the middle of the traffic." As if to make her meaning clearer, a Vespa rushed past within a few feet of them, and he smiled but didn't answer. After a moment she went on: "I think it's stimulating, somehow. It gives you a feeling of involvement—of being caught up with everything that's going on around you."

"And you find that soothing—just at the moment." It was a statement of fact rather than a question, and this time it was she who said nothing in reply. "To lose oneself in things that don't concern one, to fill one's ears with sounds that don't matter, so that one cannot hear the sounds that are important . . . there can be a great peace in that, sometimes."

Candy looked across at him with surprise and a touch of confusion—how much *had* he guessed about her?— but by this time the café proprietor had arrived with the chocolate, and he was engaged in paying for it. When the man had gone he smiled at her, and urged her to try the steaming beverage while it was still hot.

"I am waiting to hear what you think of our *cioccolata*," he remarked. "And when you have told me that, you must also tell me how you enjoyed your singing this morning."

She tasted the chocolate and burnt her tongue, but blinked the tears out of her eyes and told him it was delicious. "It really is. I didn't know it could be like that. In England it isn't very interesting."

"But here it is a speciality of the country." He stared across the road at a group of American tourists who were clustering round a jeweller's shop. "How did you find Lorenzo Galleo?"

71

She took another sip of the chocolate, and put her cup down slowly. "He was very kind," she said truthfully. "He gave me confidence."

"He would do. You pleased him?"

"I don't really know. Perhaps—I think perhaps I did." She hesitated for a moment, and then repeated what Signor Galleo had said. "He told me I must work very hard—that's what I want to do. And he said...." She broke off.

"Yes? What did he say?" He was still watching the American tourists as if their apparently unending debate on the question of whether or not to buy a souvenir interested him far more than she did, and she felt suddenly relaxed.

"He said I must give my heart to my work ... that I must lose myself in it. He said that if I wanted to be an —an artist I couldn't be an ordinary human being as well." She stopped, colouring slightly, and wondered why she had had to say so much. Whether or not she gave her heart to her work, it was nothing to do with the Conte di Lucca.

The American tourists had moved away along the street, and his attention having been released he looked across at her.

"That is excellent advice," he remarked. "Have some more chocolate."

"No, thank you. It was absolutely delicious, but I've had enough."

"You are not—what is the word—slimming?"

She laughed. "Oh, no."

"I am relieved. In such an insubstantial person it would be alarming, I think. You might disappear altogether." A half smile played around his lips, and he seemed to study her consideringly from behind the dark glasses. "You will not be homesick in Rome, I hope."

She shook her head. "I don't think so."

"Good." He hesitated a moment. "You know of course that your friend John Ryland is here?"

Afterwards Candy was not certain whether or not she had actually started. All she did know was that suddenly the light breeze that had been stirring the table-cloths and playing with the ends of her hair was almost cold, and the lively bustle of the colourful Roman street irritated her a little. Some of its strength seemed to go out of the sun, and hurriedly finishing the cold dregs of her chocolate for the sake of something to do she decided that they tasted bitter.

"No," she admitted, "I didn't know."

For several moments the Conte didn't say anything, and she felt that his eyes were penetrating her soul. And then he shrugged. "You will see him soon, I expect."

A short time later they got up to go, and he asked her if there was anything she would like to do or see during what was left of the morning.

"There is scarcely time for St. Peter's, but we could perhaps go to the Piazza di Spagna. It is near here, and there will be flower-sellers.... He hesitated, waiting possibly for her to betray some sign of enthusiasm. "On a bright winter morning there is nowhere more pleasant."

"I'm taking up too much of your time...." She felt dazed, as if the information that had just been passed on to her about John Ryland had had almost the effect of a physical blow. She scarcely knew what the man beside her was talking about, but she did understand that he was offering her a choice between remaining in his company for a while longer and being taken back to Caterina Marchetti's flat, there to be left to her own devices, and she suddenly knew that whatever happened she didn't want to be alone. Not just at the moment.

"Thank you," she said. "I'd love to see—to see. . . ."

"To see the Piazza di Spagna? I am glad."

He suggested that they should walk, and as he guided her through the laughing, hurrying crowds that packed the pavements, he pointed out everything that he thought would interest her. He was a good guide, and although the babel of bewildering sound that ebbed and flowed around them prevented her from hearing everything he said she heard enough to realize that he knew his city very well indeed. The Piazza di Spagna was the ancient square dominated by the graceful height of the Spanish Steps, and during the nineteenth century, her companion told her, it had been the favourite haunt of nearly all the British and American artists who at that time flocked to Rome. He told her how they had used the colourful figures of the flower-sellers for models, paying them very well, sometimes, to pose in picturesque attitudes amid the profuse brilliance of their flower baskets, or against the soaring honey-coloured *campanili* of Santa Maria Maggiore, the church at the top of the steps. He pointed out the house where Keats died, the famous English tea-room which had consoled genera-tions of English exiles . . . the graceful bulk of the Renaissance palaces, and the worn cobbles under their feet that had once echoed to the ring of thoroughbred hooves and the rumble of princely coach wheels. In the eighteenth century, the Conte said, the Piazza di Spagna had been one great parking place for the ponderous equipages of the nobility. As he said it, Candy recollected that he himself was a part of that nobility, and glancing up for a moment at his thin, classically perfect features she found herself wondering just how much of the old dark soul of Rome lurked behind that shuttered, unreadable face.

All at once she realized that he was asking her where she would like to go for lunch, and with a shock it occurred to her that he seemed to think it was his duty to entertain her for the rest of the day. Feeling a flush creep into her cheeks, she thanked him enthusiastically for giving her a wonderful morning.

"But now you've got to leave me to my own devices. I'd rather like to wander about by myself. Well, I mean. . . ." She floundered awkwardly.

"You would prefer to be alone?" His soft voice was neither surprised nor hurt. It was just completely expressionless.

"No, of course not." She shook her hair back from her face in a gesture that had recently become a nervous habit. "It's just that I'm being a nuisance to you."

"You are not a nuisance," he said seriously. He bent his head to study her, and a faint smile began to play about his lips. "Listen, Signorina Candida, you must be honest with me. Do you wish to be alone, or is it only that you think I do?"

She found herself smiling back. "No," she admitted, "I don't want to be alone—particularly."

"Then be kind, and spend the day with me." He spoke whimsically, but there was a kind of undercurrent

75

beneath the words—could it, she thought, be an undercurrent of loneliness?—that made her look at him rather quickly. And then she smiled wryly at the absurdity of the idea. He was titled, good-looking, extremely well-off and apparently unburdened with a wife—his problem was much more likely to be the difficulty of getting a moment to himself. Nevertheless, probably because he felt sorry for her, he seemed genuinely anxious that she should accept his offer of lunch, and she knew she couldn't obstinately persist in refusing without being positively rude.

They went to a small but obviously excellent restaurant in the shadow of St. Peter's—which the Conte promised Candy she should see in detail after lunch, or as soon after lunch as she should feel equal to it—and there, despite an almost non-existent appetite she struggled to do reasonable justice to very well prepared ravioli and veal *alla Milanese*, while her companion talked knowledgeably and entertainingly about the glories and horrors of the story of Rome, and every so often their ear-drums were assailed by a melodious, world-shaking clangour of bells.

After lunch they walked in the afternoon sunlight through the splendour of Bernini's colonnade and into the great basilica itself, and as they passed beneath the portico and paused for a moment on the edge of the glowing interior Candy caught her breath. In one of the chapels a visiting priest was saying Mass, and the murmurous intonation of the ritual was like the living echo of two thousand years of faith. They walked forward, towards the great High Altar with its towering canopy of bronze, and she felt as if she were drowning in beauty and vastness. Even the air she breathed seemed vaguely electric, as if the wonder and penitence and gratitude of the multitudinous faithful kept it charged with an ecstasy of emotion, and all around the unending whisper and rustle of humanity reminded her that for millions upon millions around the world this spot was second only to Jerusalem as a centre of pilgrimage.

Candy felt bewildered and shaken and dazzled, for it was all too much to take in at once. She stood staring in front of her with something of the awed fascination of a child, and after a moment Michele di Lucca gently put his fingers beneath her arm and guided her on again until they stood beneath the echoing vaulted magnificence of the huge dome itself.

"Look up!" he said quietly. "It is one of the sights of the world. Look up!"

She obeyed, and then gave a little gasp. "Oh!"

Above her head the glowing magnificence of Michelangelo's masterpiece soared into incalculable distance—or, at least, to her it seemed incalculable. Its hugeness and the incredible symmetry of the design on which those long-dead craftsmen had tirelessly poured out their skill amazed her, and as she gazed upwards the jewel-clear colours, gilded by sunlight, dazzled her, so that she had to blink and look away.

"Some people," said the Conte, "find St. Peter's much smaller and less impressive than they have expected it to be. Others find it great and beautiful and inspiring beyond anything they could have imagined. I think that you are of the second sort."

77

"Yes." The word sounded almost like a sigh. "Oh, yes."

They spent nearly another half hour breathing in the incense-laden tranquillity of St. Peter's, and because there was so much to see, and Candy, entranced and bewildered, lingered so long over everything it was not until they were practically on the point of leaving that they came to a standstill at last before the majestic bronze figure of Peter before which countless thousands of pilgrims down the centuries have paid homage. As they stood watching, an unending stream of men and women approached the statue, and although at first Candy couldn't see what they were doing it wasn't long before she understood. As each person stepped forward, he or she quickly bent and kissed the statue's half extended right foot. In every case the gesture was completed very swiftly and unobtrusively, and it was difficult to study the faces of the pilgrims as they went forward, but something in their very movements conveyed a little of what they were feeling. Some of them were old, some very young . . . some wore smart English or American clothes, others the dusty black of the Mediterranean peasant, but for all of them this was obviously the supreme moment. As they kissed the gleaming foot of the Apostle they fulfilled a sacred duty, and attained a grace and benediction that sent them away with shining eyes and a new lightness in their step.

Before they turned away, Michele di Lucca pointed out that the toes of the bronze foot had been almost worn out of existence by the lips of the faithful.

Outside on the steps, Candy shook her head a little,

as if to clear it. She had seen too much—too much for one day, and a strange sort of emotional exhaustion was sweeping over her. Michele looked at her shrewdly, and lightly put a hand beneath her arm.

"We'll go back to the car."

When they got back to his car he held the door open for her, and with relief she climbed inside. As he got in beside her he looked at her a little quizzically. "All right?" he enquired.

She nodded.

He let in the clutch, and they drew away from the kerb. "I was afraid," he remarked, "that you were going to faint. You are too sensitive, I think, to the influence of emotion."

She laughed, feeling faintly embarrassed. "I'm not usually overcome. But I've never seen anything quite like St. Peter's before."

"I think perhaps it is more that you have never *felt* anything like it before."

"Yes. I can't describe it, but—"

"No one can describe it. It is enough to have experienced it." He turned his head to glance at her, and she saw the rare, extraordinarily attractive smile that transformed his face. "And now it is time that you relaxed a little. I am taking you to my mother's house."

"Your mother's house? But you mustn't—well, inflict me on your mother."

Very much as if he hadn't heard her speak at all, he went on: "I am very anxious for you to meet my mother. She is an interesting person."

Candy abandoned protest. "Is she?"

"She is a film actress." He turned again to look at

the girl beside him, and this time his smile was a little peculiar. "She's very beautiful—a *femme fatale*, you could say."

It seemed rather an odd way of describing one's mother, Candy thought—although she was prepared to accept the possibility that in exalted Roman society things might be a bit different.

"I expect I've seen her. In films, I mean," she said a little awkwardly.

"Perhaps you have. She doesn't use her own name in her—in her career." It wasn't bitterness, but more a kind of bleak distaste that turned down the corners of his mouth. "You would know her as Anna Landi."

"Anna Landi!" She almost jumped. "Your mother is Anna Landi?"

"Yes."

"I—I've seen her dozens of times. I think she's a wonderful actress. I saw her in *Thunder Doesn't Last*, only a few weeks ago. She's fantastically beautiful. She can't be. . . ."

"You were going to say that she cannot be very old?" He smiled. "Well, she is not old, of course. When she married my father she was still very young, and that was not such a terribly long time ago. But still she is older than she would like to be. Time is a cruel master, *signorina*—if one allows oneself to be a slave to it."

It was obvious that the Conte di Lucca disliked his mother's chosen occupation intensely, and Candy found herself wondering exactly how well—or how badly— they got on with one another. She tried to remember exactly what Anna Landi looked like, but couldn't recall more than a general impression of dramatic dark-eyed loveliness. She knew, though, that it would be difficult to imagine her having a son of the Conte's age.

After driving for about twenty minutes through the mounting traffic of late afternoon they came out on a very broad, very straight road which was obviously leading them out of the city. A short time later their surroundings became less urban, and stone pines and cypress trees appeared along the edges of the road. Beyond the trees there were large houses, some of them apparently old and others very new, and some of the houses were sheltered by high garden walls over which bougainvillea ran riot and behind which, here and there, more cypress trees showed their slim, dark, elegant heads.

The road itself aroused Candy's curiosity, for every now and then its smooth, well-levelled tarmac surface gave way to what looked remarkably like paving-stones, and at these points it was positively bumpy. She was just about to ask the Conte why what seemed to be one of the main highways leading out of Rome had apparently been neglected by the road-menders when he took one hand off the steering-wheel to include the road stretching ahead of them and the whole of their surroundings in one expressive gesture.

"It is the Appian Way," he told her, and his voice held the mystical pride of a Roman.

The sinking sun slanted across the old road, turning its surface to dusty gold, and here and there the cypresses showed starkly black against the deepening flush in the sky.

"The Road to the South," Candy murmured, and her voice was husky.

"Yes. It was along this road that the Legions marched when they set out to take ship for Africa and Asia . . . and it was along this same way that they came when they returned, bearing their dead and wounded, and laden with marble and gold and all the treasures of the South and East to beautify the temples of Rome."

In the unearthly light of the early winter sunset everything around them seemed to quiver slightly, and to Candy it seemed that a haze of unreality veiled the cypresses and the dusty pines, and even the broad paved roadway itself. The houses on either side of them were like ghostly palaces conjured up by a dream, and the splendid wrought-iron doorways set in some of the walls were enchanted portals leading to 'faery lands forlorn'.

And then a Vespa with a faulty engine flashed past them in a searing burst of sound, ending a brief lull in the traffic, and braking gently Michele di Lucca swung his car across the road and under a wide archway on the left-hand side.

It was an archway flanked on either side by thick dark curtains of purple bougainvillea, and its wide open iron gates had a delicate beauty such as Candy had never seen in her life before. They passed between the gates with a gentle hiss of tyres, and then, within moments, came to rest in the shadow of a house.

Looking up, Candy saw high stone walls and row upon row of shuttered windows, and a kind of nervousness made her stomach turn over. And then she saw that by the steps leading up to an imposing front door another car was parked, and a man and a woman were standing beside it, talking.

The woman was very well dressed, and her beautiful dark head was held with a certain kind of defiant poise that could probably only have been acquired on the stage or in front of the cameras. The man was tall and dark, and for a moment Candy supposed that he was another Italian.

And then he turned to look at the new arrivals, and a queer little icy thrill went through her, as if she had been hit by an unusual kind of electric shock. She would have known those tanned, regular features anywhere in the world, and if she hadn't been able to see his face she would have known him even by the way he was standing ... or by the way he bent his head a little as he turned to look at the Conte's white car.

She sat quite still, saying nothing. The Italian beside her was having trouble with the hand-brake, and it was a moment or two before he looked up. When he did she felt him stiffen slightly, and although she was staring rigidly in front of her she knew that he glanced round. And then, after a second's hesitation, he got out of the car and moved round in front of it to open her door for her.

"Come and meet my mother, *signorina*."

She shook her head, and simply because she couldn't help it, looked up at him with eyes that revealed everything.

"I can't. John...." Somewhere deep down in her throat her voice was tying itself into knots, and the words wouldn't come. John Ryland and the Contessa di Lucca were watching them with a merciful detachment, waiting for them to leave the car. John, she could tell, hadn't yet recognized her.

"I know." Michele di Lucca's voice was so soft it was barely audible. "But some time you must face him . . . it is better that it should be soon."

She shook her head, wordlessly, and he straightened and closed the car door upon her. Then she saw him walk across to the couple still standing beside the other car, and a moment or so later the lovely dark-haired woman detached herself from the little group and came hurrying over to Candy.

"You are Miss Wells?" She had one of the most enchanting feminine voices the English girl had ever heard—warm, low-pitched and a little husky, and she spoke English with a kind of mixed Italian-American accent that was surprisingly attractive. "My son has told me about you. . . ." She smiled delightfully. "But he says that just now you don't feel very well? If you would like to come inside and lie down, I will call my doctor. . . ."

"Oh, but—it's all right, thank you." She flushed a little under the older woman's scrutiny. It was good of the Conte, now engaged in occupying John's attention, to try and think up an excuse for her, but although it might have looked odd it would have been kinder if he had simply driven her away again. "I mean," feeling extraordinarily foolish, "I'm all right now."

"You are sure?" The Contessa's slender eyebrows rose, but she was still smiling. "Then come in and have a drink instead."

There was, she realized, absolutely no hope of escape, and although her legs felt like lead she forced herself to climb out of the car. And at precisely the same moment John looked straight across at her. She didn't know whether the Conte had drawn his attention to her presence, or whether he had just suddenly noticed her, but she did know that she wished the ground would open and swallow her, and for a very long time afterwards she wondered just how she managed to get through the next few minutes.

But something that she supposed was a sort of mixture of pride and emotional numbness did get her through those minutes. Feeling like a sleep-walker, she talked to John Ryland as if he really were nothing more to her than her sister's brother-in-law. She never did know exactly what he looked like during those moments, or what he said to her . . . for that matter she couldn't remember what anybody said. But eventually they all moved inside the house, and she was conscious of being urged to sink into the cloud-like depths of an enormous armchair. The chair was upholstered in green velvet, and on its arms gilded lions sprawled, reminding her ridiculously of Trafalgar Square. She was in an enormous room—a splendid room in which she had the feeling that time might stand still, past and present and future becoming fused together in a healing, soothing harmony with the power to make all life's problems seem far away and unimportant. Lofty windows lavishly draped with dark green velvet rose almost to the high, ornate ceiling, and everywhere ponderously beautiful carved furniture, heavy with marble and gilt, exuded the spirit and essence of an age that, dead almost everywhere else, in this room seemed alive and breathing.

The Conte was bending over her. "You'll have a glass of wine? Or perhaps something stronger?"

She looked up, but for a moment didn't see him. Her

mind refused to register. Then his serious eyes penetrated her consciousness, and she coloured faintly.

"Nothing, thank you."

"Not even a glass of water?" very quietly. "It would steady you."

She let him put a tall, sparkling glass of water into her hand, and was grateful for the coolness of it, and, in a vague kind of way, for his coolly considerate presence. It was obvious that he knew or had guessed all about her and John Ryland, and although at one time it would have been more than she could bear that anyone should have the power to spy on her private anguish, somehow Michele di Lucca didn't seem to matter.

She discovered that her hostess had come over to sit beside her, and was making a determined effort to engage her in conversation.

"John tells me that your sister is married to his brother." The brief, formal remark broke through the numbness surrounding Candy, and she found herself stammering a disconnected reply.

"Yes, he—my sister—I...we know one another."

"Quite well, I expect." The lovely eyes were intent. A good many people around the world would have been grateful for such an opportunity of studying Anna Landi at close quarters, but at the moment the advantages of the situation were lost on Candy.

"Yes, quite well."

"He's a very...interesting man." The Contessa turned her elegant head to take another look at her son and John Ryland, who were once again conducting a rather desultory dialogue on the other side of the room, and for the first time Candy really took in the striking quality of the older woman's beauty. She looked very little more than thirty, but it was obvious that to have a son of the Conte's age she must be at least fifteen years older than that. Her skin had a flawless, creamy perfection that was far too remarkable to be just the result of skilful make-up, and neither around her enormous eyes nor her well-moulded mouth was there a wrinkle to be seen. Her thick black hair was arranged on top of her shapely head in heavy, gleaming coils of elegance, and Candy noticed that even her beringed hands were white and supple and incredibly smooth-skinned, their long, tapering coral tips contrasting effectively with the paleness of the slender fingers.

She was speaking again, her attention temporarily diverted from the two men. "You like Rome?" she asked, leaning back to rest her head against a pile of cushions. Her eyes, half-closed and as inscrutable as a cat's, studied the English girl attentively. "You think you will find it pleasant to live here?"

"Oh, yes ... very pleasant. But I don't expect I shall be living here long."

"Why not? Your music will probably keep you here long after Signor Galleo has finished instructing you. There are many opportunities for young singers in Rome, and you would be foolish to turn your back on them. Tell me, is your singing to be your life?"

Startled by the suddenness and directness of the question, Candy hesitated. And then her decision of the morning came back to her, and as she glanced across the room and her eyes fell on John Ryland she said fervently : "Yes. Singing is everything to me—absolutely everything."

The Contessa looked at her for a moment, a tiny smile touching the corners of her mouth. And then, almost imperceptibly, she shrugged. "When we are young," she remarked cryptically, "we have the strangest ideas." With a swift movement she took the half-empty glass out of Candy's hand and set it down on a nearby table. "Something a little stronger," she re-market, "would be good for you. Michele, give Miss Wells a glass of sherry."

Reluctantly, for she didn't feel like arguing, Candy accepted the sherry, and as she sipped it her hostess leaned forward to pat her arm almost affectionately.

"To-night I am having a little dinner-party, and of course you will stay for it."

"Oh, but I couldn't !" Candy protested in genuine horror. "I mean . . . you don't know me. I'm just being a nuisance."

"But how nonsensical ! It is what Michele brought you for. You are an artist . . . and I love all artists. Please, *signorina,* I shall be very unhappy if you will not stay."

Candy wondered if John Ryland would be staying too, and her nerve almost failed her. And then pride came to her rescue, and she smiled. "Thank you, Contessa, I'd love to stay."

Shortly afterwards the older woman left her, to lean against the massive marble fireplace and talk or rather listen, to John Ryland. She seemed to be a good listener, when it suited her, and clearly it suited her to listen to the tall, dark-haired Englishman. Candy watched them, and slowly, gradually, she began to understand.

From the beginning she had noticed that John and the statuesque Italian beauty found one another interesting—that wasn't particularly surprising. But now, as she studied them both more carefully, she realized with a painful shock that there was more than interest between them. As they talked, John rarely took his eyes off the Contessa's lovely face, and even from a distance Candy could see how the actress's eyes shone luminously every time she looked up at him.

Candy sipped at her sherry, and it made her cough. So that was it! John had gone to Rome, and in Rome he had met the Contessa di Lucca—or perhaps he thought of her as Anna Landi. As a result of that meeting his life had been changed, and looking at him now as calmly and objectively as she could manage to do, she saw quite clearly that as far as he was concerned the mother of Michele di Lucca had become the centre of the world.

After a few minutes Michele himself moved over again to the English girl, and standing beside her as if he felt happier on his feet launched into a rather stiff and uninspired effort at conversation. His brown eyes seemed to stare over the top of her head, into nothingness, and she had the feeling that he was absolutely detached, for which she was thankful.

At about half past seven his mother sent for one of the maids, and she was whisked off to an enormous guest bedroom, where she was left alone to make any repairs to her appearance that she might think necessary. Despite what her hostess had said about informality she wished very much that she could have had an opportunity to change. To her it seemed extremely unlikely that any woman, given the opportunity to prepare herself properly, would turn up for dinner at such a house as the Contessa's without being dressed to suit the occasion, and that almost certainly meant formal evening dress. If she had not been in such a numb and abstracted mood she supposed she would probably have been in an agony of nervousness and apprehension, but as it was she had neither the energy nor the interest to care very much. If it had been possible for her to change she would have done so, but as it wasn't possible the light woollen dress in which she had set out that morning would undoubtedly have to do. It was an attractive dress, of navy blue with a deep band of white around the hem, and its fitted bodice and slightly flared skirt suited her insubstantial figure so well that she couldn't really have looked more enchanting if she had been dressed for the evening by Balenciaga. She didn't know that she looked enchanting, but she hadn't the heart to worry about it, and after washing quickly in an adjoining bathroom concentrated mainly on doing what she could with her face and hair.

The room in which she had been left was an artistic creation in white and gold, and despite her abstracted state of mind as soon as the door was flung open by the maid she had uttered a little gasp of pleasure. The dominant feature of the room was a gilded and incredibly pretty French bed, with a cover of heavy white silk, and in front of the half open windows long curtains of gold brocade swayed gently in a cool current of evening air. The honey-coloured floorboards were scattered with rugs of thick white fur, and there were armchairs upholstered in white velvet and piled with gold brocade cushions. The dressing-table was a massive French antique, littered with silver-stoppered bottles and jars, and reposing on its burnished surface there was even a set of heavy silver-backed brushes and combs.

Gingerly, Candy lifted one of the magnificent brushes, and then put it down again rather as if it had threatened to bite her. She opened her handbag and taking out her own comb ran it rather hastily through her hair, which actually wasn't in need of much attention, powdered her nose and outlined her forlornly drooping mouth with lipstick. Then she gathered up her bag and left the room, closing the door behind her.

Outside in the echoing marble-floored corridor she hesitated for a moment, uncertain which way to go, but then she managed to remember which way she had come with the maid, and after that it was a simple matter to retrace her steps until she came to the graceful curve of the staircase. There, however, she stopped, for just below her, in the echoing entrance hall, two people were talking, and somehow she sensed immediately that their conversation was of a sort which it could be embarrassing to overhear.

"Marco. . . ." It was the Contessa's voice, and it was husky with a kind of urgent appeal. She was speaking in Italian, rapidly and anxiously, and she was obviously making a considerable effort to be both persuasive and soothing. Hesitating at the head of the stairs, Candy looked over the gilded iron balustrade and saw that the actress was standing just below her, her dark head gleaming like burnished ebony in the light from the chandeliers. She had changed into a little gold lamé suit which bore the unmistakable stamp of one of Rome's topmost fashion houses, and as she moved her slim hands in a series of expressive gestures they flashed with the dark green fire of emeralds.

The man beside her was about the same height as herself, and his hair, which once had obviously been very black, was tinged here and there with streaks of silver. He was probably, Candy thought, about fifty, and undoubtedly Italian. His dark grey suit was very well cut, and although he was possibly a little over-weight on the whole he looked rather an elegant figure. To Candy it seemed that there was something decidedly familiar about him, and as she stared down at the top of his head she suddenly realized what it was. He was remarkably like the Conte di Lucca.

Suddenly, somewhere, a bell rang—evidently the front door bell, for a uniformed maid came hurrying to answer it—and the Contessa checked herself in what sounded like the middle of a sentence. The man, who didn't really seem to have said very much, shrugged and moved a little away from her and as he did so a man and a girl were ushered by the maid into the circle of light cast by the great central chandelier, and the woman known to the world as Anna Landi advanced to meet them with both hands outstretched.

When, several minutes after the hall had again emptied itself, Candy at last found the courage to descend the staircase and rejoin her hostess and her fellow-guests in the *salotto* with the green velvet hangings she found, more or less as she had expected, that rather a daunting little gathering had assembled in her absence.

The Contessa was perched on the arm of a sofa, engaged in an animated if one-sided conversation with a pretty black-haired girl in a long fluttering dress of eggshell blue voile, and beside the girl, on the same sofa, a massive matron in black velvet seemed to be her mother was placidly monopolizing the Conte. John Ryland, temporarily a little lost, was standing alone in front of the fireplace, staring into the rosy-hued cocktail in his glass as if it were a crystal ball, and the Italian with the greying hair whom Candy had seen with the Contessa was also alone, gazing through one of the uncurtained windows into the clear, starlit night. The couple whose arrival had interrupted his conversation with his hostess were there too, and just as Candy entered the room the man moved purposefully over to the Contessa, with the evident intention of attracting some of her attention to himself. He was tall and lean, with a slight stoop, and an American accent which could probably have been heard easily on the other side of the heavy oak door. The girl who had arrived with him was left sitting alone and looking rather bewildered, and as she glanced at her with mild curiosity Candy realized that she was from the East—possibly from Japan. She was wearing a romantically beautiful evening dress of heavy, gleaming silk in which glowing reds and golds blended luxuriantly, and everything about her small, neat figure was almost unbelievably delicate and doll-like.

On impulse, and partly because of a subconscious feeling that they were both in a sense outsiders, Candy sat down beside the little silk-clad shape and smiled at her. It didn't seem to her to matter that they hadn't been introduced, for if she was not simply to run out of the house in an agony of unhappiness and embarrassment she had to talk to somebody, and she saw nobody else to whom it would be possible to attach herself.

The girl smiled back, revealing extraordinarily pretty teeth, and in precise, slightly accented English she murmured something formal and predictable about the beauty of the room, and the excellence of the Contessa's central heating. And then to Candy's astonishment and horror, her slanting brown eyes suddenly filled with tears, and her small mouth puckered. The tears overflowed and began to roll down her cheeks, and then she started to sob audibly . . . little, subdued, choking sobs that despite their unobtrusiveness had a powerful and immediate impact on the whole of the room.

Everyone looked round as swiftly as if the girl had stood up and screamed, and one by one they all stopped talking. In the silence the two Italian women on the sofa stared across incredulously at their fellow-guest— the elder with mounting disapproval in every line of her heavy-jowled face, the younger open-mouthed and fascinated—and the men froze where they stood.

Only the Contessa remained in command of the situation. A bare half-glance had evidently been enough to allow her to take in what was happening, and once she had taken it in she tactfully avoided looking a second time. Instead, she glanced with very slightly upraised eyebrows at the girl's husband, into whose sallow cheeks a dull red flush was slowly creeping, and muttering something the American left her and walked over to his wife.

"Listen, stop it, will you?" Candy didn't want to listen, but she couldn't help overhearing the half-whispered words. The man had so placed himself that he was between the weeping girl and most of the other people present, and only Candy, who for some reason hadn't thought of moving away, saw the look in her eyes as she lifted her distorted face.

"I can't bear it!" The girl's soft voice was hoarse and choked. "I can't—not any more! Not any more, Lester. I'm telling you the truth."

"Okay, okay." He seemed to be keeping his temper in check with an effort. "Just let's get out of here. Where's your coat?" He put out a hand to pull the small, hysterical figure to her feet, but as he did so she pushed him away, and the next instant she had jumped up and almost literally flown at him, first pounding on his chest with her tiny clenched fists and then actually tearing at his startled face with her sharply pointed, silvery finger-nails.

"Why don't you get a divorce and marry her?" Her voice, thin and piercing, rising almost to a shriek, echoed around the room. "Why don't you? Why don't you? Why don't you get a divorce. . . ?"

It seemed as if the awful repetition would go on for ever. Her husband had grasped her hands in self-defence, but she seemed to be going from bad to worse. And then suddenly someone stepped forward and gently grasped her shoulders. It was the Italian to whom the Contessa had been talking in the hall, and the interference of a stranger had an instantaneous effect. All the tautness went out of the Japanese girl's body, and her hands dropped to her sides. She looked like a sleep-walker who is slowly waking up and returning to normality, and in the shocked silence that had fallen she allowed herself to be guided out of the room. Her husband ran his hands through his hair, looked at the Contessa and muttered something that sounded like a muffled apology, then followed the girl through the door and out of sight.

The silence they left behind them lasted about fifteen seconds. Then the Contessa spread her hands in a delicate gesture that would have done credit to one of her screen performances, and looked around at her remaining guests with the merest suspicion of a smile on her scarlet lips.

"Mario tells me dinner is ready. Let's go into the *sala*, shall we?"

Dinner was immensely formal, and it went on for a very long time. Shortly after the arrival of the third course Candy's head began to ache, and she wished more than anything that she could have been allowed to call a taxi, slip quietly back to Signorina Marchetti's flat and go to bed. John Ryland was seated on the Contessa's right, and they were obviously absorbed in one another —or at least, John was absorbed, and it was quite clear that the Italian beauty was very much attracted by him. Her son, Michele, discharged the duties of a host with a well-schooled courtesy which fell a little short of concealing the profound indifference with which he seemed to regard everybody and everything, but the mother and daughter who had been placed on either side of him quite obviously found him fascinating. There was little doubt that the elder of the two entertained certain hopes where her daughter and the Conte were

96

concerned, and although Candy had no means of knowing what sort of basis she had for those hopes she did
feel that if she had been the Italian girl she would have
found Michele's air of polite abstraction disconcerting,
to say the least.

As the meal wore on, the grouse imported from Scot-
land gave way to a long and slightly wearisome proces-
sion of gateaux, fruits and cheeses Candy found herself
wondering more and more about the Japanese girl. She
supposed that most of the other people present were
wondering too, and she was a little surprised that the
incident had not had a more noticeable effect upon
John. The girl had obviously been jealous of the attention being paid by her husband to the beautiful Anna,
and everything she said and did had suggested that
there was more than a passing flirtation involved. It
was true that the Contessa herself had appeared to be
supremely indifferent to both of them, and it was also
true that the man had not really seemed to be on very
close terms with his hostess. But there had certainly been
something.... Didn't John feel even a twinge of
curiosity—of resentment? Candy was surprised to find
that she could now take a kind of detached interest in
analysing his feelings, and she looked at him. He was
gazing into the beautiful dark eyes so close to his own
with a smile on his face that she had never seen before,
and it occurred to her that he closely resembled the
object of an experiment in hypnotism.

"You are very silent, *signorina*."

It was the middle-aged Italian who had been so
successful in sorting out the explosive situation in the
salotto, and she turned to smile at him. Although they

were seated side by side they hadn't so far talked very much, for she had a strong feeling that, like herself and the Conte, he wasn't really in the mood for conversation, but now she supposed that it was time she made an effort.

"I was thinking what a wonderful room this is." It was partly true, for the Contessa's marble dining-room was everything her green *salotto* led one to expect.

"You think this house is beautiful?"

"Of course—very beautiful."

"You should see the Palazzo Lucca. It is one of the bright jewels of the Renaissance." He glanced along the table at Michele. "Unfortunately, it belongs now to my nephew...." So that was it. She had realized he was a relative, but not that he was the Conte's uncle. "He is young and unmarried, and has use for nothing but a corner of it, so the rest is shut up. Tell me, *signorina*, don't you think my nephew should marry?"

She hesitated, for some reason finding the question faintly embarrassing. "Well, yes ... of course. But I don't suppose it will be very long—"

"No?" he interrupted. He glanced at the girl in pale blue voile, whose slanting sloe-like eyes were fixed on Michele's face as if her life depended on not missing a flicker of his eyelids, and automatically Candy looked in the same direction. "That one, do you think? Her father is a Milanese industrialist, with more money than even her mother can find a use for, and she has had the very best education."

"Well...." Candy said again, and her companion laughed and tilted his wine glass to admire the glowing crimson of its contents.

"Don't listen to me, Miss Wells. I have drunk too much this evening, and before I go home I shall drink more . . . a lot more. I am—how do you say it?—the black sheep of the di Lucca family."

She turned to look at him with interest. As far as she knew she had never met a 'black sheep' before, and she wasn't really in a position to judge, but she wouldn't have said, if she had been asked, that this ageing, benevolent Italian looked at all the type.

"I don't think you're very black," she said, and smiled.

"Thank you, my little one." Her hand was lying on the table, and he put his wine-glass down and patted it. "You are undoubtedly the princess in the fairy-story who turns frogs into princes . . . a refreshing addition to my sister-in-law's weary circle of friends." He turned his head away from her, and she saw that he was gazing at John Ryland as if he felt that some other recent additions were rather less refreshing.

After dinner, back in the splendid green *salotto*, John continued to monopolize his hostess more or less completely, and the Italian mother-and-daughter team continued to occupy the Conte. Marco di Lucca disappeared, and all at once Candy found herself quite alone. She walked over to one of the high windows, and cautiously parted the curtains. Outside the night was clear and starlit, with just a trace of light wind to shake the rustling palm fronds and stir the dark heads of the cypresses. It was beautiful and romantic, and it made her want to cry. Behind her, in the room, she could hear John's voice talking to the Contessa—during the whole of the evening he had scarcely addressed a word to her, Candy—and the desolation which she had thought she could put behind her by absorbing herself in her new work and ambitions came rushing over her again, swamping her with misery, flooding her entire being with an abject dejection that actually seemed to drain her strength way—to rob her of the energy she needed to cope with life. Enormous tears forced their way beneath her eyelids and cascaded silently down her cheeks, and but for the fact that her sense of utter isolation made her feel almost that she was alone in the room she would have been paralysed with horror. As it was, it simply didn't occur to her that someone might suddenly decide to find out what she was doing with herself, and when all at once a voice just behind her spoke her name her heart jumped very nearly into her throat.

"Candida!" It was the first time Michele had made use of her Christian name, and despite the horror of the moment she rather liked the way he said it. But the next instant all she was conscious of was a bitter shame and confusion that seemed to emanate from her soul.

"I didn't know you were there," she said foolishly.

"Would you like me to go away?"

"N-no. Of course not." She hadn't looked at him, and it occurred to her that perhaps he hadn't noticed her damp cheeks yet—perhaps, if she were careful, he wouldn't notice them. But the next instant this idea was shattered.

"You can't cry here," he said quietly. "That is"—a whimsical note entering his voice—"some people, of course, can and do, but I think you would rather be somewhere else. Come and see my mother's music-room."

Meekly, like a child, she let him usher her out of the *salotto*, and she didn't think anyone even noticed their departure. He took her along a wide, carpeted, softly-lit corridor leading towards the back of the house, and then they turned out of the first corridor into another. Finally they arrived at a pair of double doors made of dully gleaming mahogany, and as she entered the room that lay beyond them its warm tranquillity came to meet her, actually causing her to stand still and draw a shuddering breath, as if something vital inside her were relaxing.

"Would you like me to leave you here?" The Conte's voice had something curiously gentle about it, but it also sounded essentially matter-of-fact.

She shook her head slowly, and turned to look at him, now, without caring in the least that her cheeks were still wet and her make-up probably smudged. She even managed a slightly shaky smile. "I'm not going to cry any more. But thank you for getting me away from . . . all those people. This room makes me feel better. It's got a wonderful atmosphere." She hesitated. "But I think I'd like to go now—if you don't mind. If you could call me a taxi—and say good-bye to—to your mother for me. . . ?"

He looked into her face with a kind of dispassionate curiosity, and then he lightly touched her shoulder.

"I won't keep you here if you would prefer to go, but I thought—perhaps you might like to stay for a while." He paused for a moment, and when he spoke again it was almost as if he were bringing the words out with difficulty. "Sometimes—when one is suffering—music draws out the sting ... relieves the pain." He stopped again. "For me it is so, and I thought that perhaps for you to. ..."

She looked at him, and this time it was her turn to feel curiosity. His face had a hollow look, and his mouth was set in lines of inexpressible bleakness. She remembered that the weary melancholy in his eyes had been the first thing she had noticed about him, and, suddenly jolted out of herself, she found herself wondering what it was that had etched those marks in his face, and whether, whatever it was, it now lay buried in the past. Or whether, perhaps, it was still being endured.

"There's my mother's piano," he was saying. "And there are hundreds of records. I'll leave you here ... you might be able to amuse yourself."

"No. ..." She hesitated. "Please don't—there's no need for you to go." On impulse she added, "I'd love to hear you play something." If he had been any other man she couldn't have said it, but with him, at this moment, she had no feeling of selfconsciousness. Only an awareness that in this room, and in his presence, there was immeasurable peace.

For several seconds he said nothing, merely looking at her. And then, still in silence, he walked over to the beautiful, dark, gleaming grand piano at the far end of the room, and started to sift through a pile of music. Candy sank into a chair, and, relaxed, set her senses free to absorb the room's rather sombre, old-fashioned charm.

The carpet was a dull crimson colour, and so thick that every sound was muffled in its velvety depths. The curtains were crimson, too, and they hung in thick, heavy folds before unseen windows that she supposed were as tall as those in the *salotto*. The ceiling was very high, but efficient central heating kept the whole room warm, and there was an extraordinary cosiness about it. All the furniture was of dark mahogany, and wherever the walls were not obscured by shelf after shelf of records and sheet music they were covered in crimson brocade.

Michele had opened the piano and sat down in front of it, and slowly and gently the first notes of Beethoven's Moonlight Sonata stole on to the atmosphere. The Sonata was followed by a Chopin waltz, and then a nocturne. . . . Candy sat listening with the keenest, most acute pleasure, and not only that, but a very real feeling of being temporarily anaesthetized against every hurt that life could offer. He finished with the plaintive beauty of Brahms' Cradle Song, and when he stopped she wanted to ask him to go on—to go on and on, and keep the soothing flow of melody running for ever.

But she didn't, and he closed the piano and turned round. "You feel better?" He was smiling.

"Much better." She stood up. "Thank you. And now I'll have to go." Her eyes, very green in the lamplight, smiled into his with sudden warmth. "You're kind," she said, almost without thinking.

He shook his head slowly. "No. Not kind."

The Conte insisted on driving her back to Miss Marchetti's flat, and as soon as she had said good-bye to her hostess—who enveloped her in a haze of expensive French perfume as she kissed her rather theatrically on both cheeks—they walked out to his car, still waiting on the gravel sweep before the imposing front door. When he had closed the door on Candy and climbed into the driving seat he lit a cigarette, and Candy felt mildly surprised, for she had never seen him smoke before. As if he felt the surprise he glanced round at her in the faint light from the newly switched on head-lamps, and she sensed something oddly rueful in his face.

"I don't smoke often," he said suddenly. "But some-times. . . . It is a bad habit—very bad." He ground the cigarette out in the ash-tray in front of him, and turned the key in the ignition. The car swung almost silently back through the gates and under the old stone arch-way, and soon they were speeding back along the Appian Way. Michele said nothing for several minutes, and then he spoke abruptly.

"I am very sorry . . . about this evening!"

Under cover of the darkness Candy flushed. "There's nothing to be sorry about," she said awkwardly. "I—I had a wonderful evening. Your mother is—"

"My mother is a notorious man-hunter. And her latest victim is—happens to be someone who is im-portant to you, no?"

"*Was* important to me," Candy said quickly, feeling the colour still burning in her cheeks, the tears threaten-ing again behind her eyelids.

"No. One day," gently, "you will say that. But not yet."

For some time they were both silent, and then, as they paused at a busy crossroads near the centre of Rome, he spoke again. "You saw Mrs. Endacombe?" he asked.

"Mrs. Endacombe?"

"She is Japanese, although married to an American diplomat. "I think," rather drily, "you certainly saw her to-night."

"Oh . . . Yes, of course."

"James Endacombe has been a—close friend of my mother's. You will have guessed that."

Embarrassed, Candy said nothing.

"Their relationship is now over. I don't know why he takes his wife to the house. It could be that he wishes to torture her, but I think it is more a form of stupidity. They are to pretend—she is to pretend—that nothing has happened. But what I wanted to make clear is that with my mother things do end. One day your friend John Ryland will go his own way, and she will go hers."

When they got back to the flat Caterina Marchetti was waiting for them, but although he greeted her with what looked to Candy like indulgent affection Michele firmly refused her offer of a cup of coffee, and said good-night to both of them at the ground-floor entrance to the flats. He had gone back to his car, and was just about to climb into the driving-seat when he suddenly turned and came hurrying back to speak to Candy. She was just about to enter the lift with Caterina when he caught up with them, and the Italian woman looked rather amused.

"There is something I forgot to say to Candida," he explained. "It is about her work."

"Very well." With a surprising absence of rancour Caterina patted the English girl's arm and stepped back into the lift. "I will go ahead, *cara*, and prepare the coffee."

When they were alone Candy noticed that in the rather harsh light of the lobby the Conte seemed to look more drawn than ever, and with a sudden uprush of sympathy for him Candy wished she knew what it was that made him look like that. She wished she knew whether it would be possible to help him.

"I came back," he told her, "to say something that I meant to say to you earlier." He paused. "You were distressed to-night."

She looked away from him, and he apologized swiftly. "Forgive me. I didn't wish to hurt you—to constantly remind you. It was only that I wondered if you realized —if you understood how much your music could help you."

"Yes," she said rather wearily. "Signor Galleo said a lot about that."

"Did he? I think you will find it is true."

"I expect I shall." This time she definitely sounded tired and withdrawn.

"What I wanted to say to you is that I think you should absorb yourself in your singing as much as possible." He hesitated. "I know something of music. In between your lessons with Galleo I could perhaps help you. . . ."

She looked up at him quickly, and there was a glow of real gratitude in her eyes as she thanked him.

"Would you really? I do need someone to—to just sort of *listen* to me. . . ." And then she broke off. "Oh, but I couldn't expect you to bother—"

"I suggested it," he reminded her coolly. "So you can

certainly expect me to bother. Caterina has a piano here. I will not disturb her to-night, but in the morning I will telephone her, and we will arrange everything." He smiled at her with the sudden brilliance that she had seen in his face only once or twice before. "Does it please you?"

"It's wonderful. I'm so grateful."

For several seconds he looked into her face. "There is no need," he said gently, "to talk of being grateful. Good-night, Candida."

And then he was gone, and she hurried upstairs in the lift to join Caterina Marchetti.

CHAPTER SEVEN

IN the morning Michele telephoned as he had promised, and as it happened Lorenzo Galleo telephoned too. Between them they worked out a programme for Candy that looked like leaving her with very little time for anything but music in the weeks immediately ahead, and she was grateful to them both. She was very grateful, too, to Miss Marchetti, who entered into the spirit of the thing with warm enthusiasm, and placed her own drawing-room with its beautiful Bechstein piano at Candy's disposal almost whenever she wanted it. Candy realized, of course, that the Italian woman was probably glad of the opportunity to see such a lot of Michele, and she supposed too that Michele was equally happy about this aspect of the situation, although she was quite prepared to believe he felt a genuine wish to help her, Candy. There was, she decided, something very attractive about the Conte's personality. She hoped he and Caterina would make up their minds about one another soon.

November passed, and the first two weeks of December, and all at once Christmas was almost upon them, and Candy realized that for the first time in her life she would be spending the festive season outside England. She was half prepared for a sharp bout of homesickness, but as the days went by everyone around her seemed to conspire to see to it that she hardly had time for lingering thoughts of snow and holly and mince pies. With Caterina she went Christmas shopping in the smart shops of modern Rome, buying presents for Sue and her brother-in-law and the children, and—because they were so beautiful and she couldn't resist them—far more Christmas cards than she could possibly find a use for.

Caterina seemed to buy mountains of expensive gifts, from enormous bottles of perfume to an enchanting velvet-covered teddy bear intended for a very small cousin, and Christmas was obviously a time of the year that delighted her. Her pleasure in every sort of preparation was almost childlike, and Candy, who had grown genuinely fond of her in the course of the last few weeks, felt glad that they would be spending most of the holiday together. Caterina was not going away—her parents were dead and her only brother was in America—and when Candy had at one time tried to insist upon removing herself from the Italian woman's flat for the second half of December she had been genuinely horrified. She had, of course, been invited to an enormous number of parties, and to Candy's amazement she, too, had been anything but overlooked. Lorenzo Galleo and his wife had urged her if she had nothing else to do to spend at least part of Christmas Day with them at their flat near the Via Veneto, and numerous Italian women whom she had met over the past few weeks had sent her invitations to social gatherings, while for Christmas Eve itself there was rather a special invitation. Both she and Caterina had been asked to have dinner on that evening at the Casa Lucca,

Michele's reputedly splendid Renaissance *palazzo* in the heart of the old city.

Just under a week before Christmas, Caterina unexpectedly asked her English guest if she would like to go with her to the Convent of the Holy Angels. "Today," she explained, "the Sisters have a party for all the poor children of their district. Every year I go— just to help a little, and to watch." Her dark eyes smiled. "With so many children there is a lot to watch."

When they got to the old, stone-walled convent, it seemed to Candy that for this one afternoon at least the whole building had been thrown open to all the children in Rome. The nuns' long dining-hall had been transformed into a fairyland, with tinsel and paper-chains and huge boughs of evergreen in all directions, and along the walls trestle tables laden with cakes, jellies, sandwiches and big bowls of *pasta* were obviously exercising such a fascination for hundreds of pairs of small dark eyes that there seemed every possibility of a stampede if supervision should not be adequate. Supervision, however, was adequate, and in fact it seemed to Candy that the Sisters' skill with such a fantastic assortment of urchins was positively miraculous. Some of the children, it was explained to her, came from the poorest and roughest homes in that part of the city, and under normal circumstances their manners probably matched their backgrounds. But the mere fact that they were under the Convent roof seemed to have a powerful effect upon them, and although they were obviously enjoying themselves very few of them gave any trouble.

Candy was enchanted by them—by their small, olive-tinted faces and their silky black curls, their long, sweeping eyelashes and the delicate features that in so many cases bore the unmistakable stamp of old Rome, and in her broken Italian she tried to talk to some of them. They were certainly quite willing to talk to her, and here and there she managed to understand a lot. They nearly all belonged to big families—one little boy claimed proudly that he had eight brothers and six sisters—and most of them went to school. The Holy Virgin and the good Sisters played an important part in their conversation and, apparently, in their lives, and some of the saints seemed as familiar to them as members of their own families. They weren't curious about Candy—they had seen foreign *signorine* before—but they were curious about the small presents hanging in clusters on the tall Christmas tree by the door.

Eventually, when practically all the *pasta* and the cakes and the jellies had been consumed, but everybody's eyes were still fastened on the tree, two of the nuns set upon it and solemnly divested it of its colourful burdens. Then the interesting packages were carefully distributed so that not a single child was left out, and for ten minutes there really was a kind of controlled pandemonium. Each child had one box of sweets and one package containing a toy, and there were shrieks of delight in all directions as cuddly stuffed animals, small vehicles of every description and diminutive sets of dolls' furniture cascaded over the floor like something out of a child's Christmas dream.

"Everybody gives, so that there is enough for them all," Caterina Marchetti said softly. "Once," she added, "it was the custom to give them things to wear—shoes and gloves, and jumpers of wool. But the Reverend Mother decided it was more important that they should be given something which would make them truly happy ... just once in the year." Her face softened. "They have so few toys."

The distribution of presents, however, was not the ultimate climax of the afternoon, and after a reasonable interval had been allowed for gloating over new acquisitions the nuns called for silence. One of them started speaking in Italian, and Caterina turned to her English companion with a slightly guilty expression on her face.

"Candy, I did not tell you before, but—at the end of the Christmas party it is the custom to sing. Hymns, you know, and one or two songs of the kind children like. Some of the nuns have good voices, but this is not quite the sort of thing they are used to. So ..." she smiled apologetically, "I told them you would lead them!"

After the first shock of discovering what was expected of her, and of realizing that she couldn't possibly get out of it, Candy began to enjoy herself more than she would have believed possible. She had never done anything of the sort in her life before, and for a few moments, as she went over to stand beside the small bespectacled nun who was seated in front of the piano, she felt decidedly shy, for the suddenly solemn eyes of what looked like several hundred Italian children were fixed exclusively on her, and every one of the Sisters seemed to be regarding her with exactly the same smile of gentle expectation. But the little nun at the piano began to play immediately, and she discovered to her relief that the hymns to be sung were all more or less familar to her. And although she sang in English while the nuns and children sang in Italian, somehow the mixing of the languages didn't seem to matter. They sang *Away in a Manger* and *Hark! the Herald Angels Sing*, and she was amazed to discover how many of the hymns she had always thought of as belonging to the Church of England were apparently well known to Roman Catholics. Then there were the songs that had been selected for her. These she was expected to sing more or less solo, but the nuns joined in here and there, and in any case she knew all the songs well, and her confidence increased by leaps and bounds. The children didn't understand English, but they were none the less appreciative for that, and as she progressed from *Rudolf the Red-Nosed Reindeer* to *Little Donkey* and *Mary's Boy Child* they became raptly attentive.

Although Candy's whole training was tending towards the preservation of her voice for opera and fairly serious music she was not at all the sort of singer who finds it impossible to cope with an ordinary, catchy melody, and as she stood between the piano and the Christmas tree, in the stone-flagged dining-hall of the convent, singing the songs of Christmas for the entertainment of poor Roman children she felt her spirit lightening, and a new warmth and energy pervading her voice.

As the last notes of *Mary's Boy Child* died away on the piano the little plump Sister leant towards Candy, her eyes sparkling behind her rimless spectacles, and whispered that it would be nice if they could now have *Silent Night*. Candy agreed enthusiastically, and as if at a pre-arranged signal two of the novices went round the room turning practically all the lights out. The children were beckoned closer, and Candy began. By now she had lost every trace of self-consciousness, and her voice, clear and pure and incredibly soft, had a breathtaking quality about it.

"*Silent night, holy night ... all is calm, all is bright.*" The nuns folded their arms about their white-robed figures, and their tranquil faces beamed.

Carried away by her singing, Candy didn't notice that one of the main doors to the passage way had opened, and at first she didn't see the new arrival who had slipped unobtrusively into the room and taken up his position behind a cluster of novices. She had reached the second verse, and was beginning to be conscious of a faint prickling behind the eyelids at the thought, suddenly conjured up, of half-forgotten childhood Christmases when her attention was attracted by a movement, and she saw Michele di Lucca. He was standing in the shadows watching her, and in an odd way the sight of him was a shock. Her voice wavered, throwing the pianist into temporary confusion, and although she recovered quickly and went on more or less as before she knew that all the adults present were looking at her in mild surprise. All, that is, except the Conte, whose dimly seen face looked unreadable.

"*Christ the Saviour is born. ...*" Softly and sweetly, her voice died away on the familiar last words of the carol, and as the hushed piano also faded into silence she was startled and embarrassed by an eager, spontaneous burst of applause.

"That was *bellissima, signorina.*" It was Reverend Mother, coming towards her with hands outstretched.

"And now we will have *Adeste Fideles*, and you will lead us."

The little nun struck a resounding chord on the piano, and everybody stood. Slowly, and with as much feeling as she could infuse into it, Candy sang *O Come, All Ye Faithful* as she knew it, and all around her Italian voices, young and old, joined in. The surge of sound was melodious and heart-warming, the sound of Christmas itself, pure and simple and unchanging, and this time, as she sang the last note she knew that her cheeks were wet.

Again the piano fell silent, and in the stillness that followed Candy felt all the exhilaration she had been feeling seep out of her, to be succeeded by a wave of dejection so overpowering that it seemed to her she was physically crushed by it. All her energy drained away from her, and all at once felt bitterly lonely ... utterly isolated. The childhood memories mocked her for a moment, and then receded. She looked around for Caterina, but somehow she couldn't see her. Instead she saw the Conte di Lucca, and he was coming towards her.

Afterwards she had a vague recollection of the white-clad Sisters crowding round her, thanking her and congratulating her, and she remembered too that one of the little girls was deputed to present her with a small, neat bouquet—a bunch of hothouse roses. But the only thing she was really clear about was the fact that she had felt completely exhausted and extraordinarily miserable, and that the only person it had been possible to lean on was Michele di Lucca.

She didn't know what happened to Caterina—at the

time it didn't occur to her to wonder—but she did know that very quickly she found herself outside in the narrow street with Michele. It was a cool, starlit evening, and somewhere bells were beginning to clang for Benediction. Not attempting to pretend, she leant against the stone wall of the convent, and passed a hand across her forehead.

"I suppose it was too hot in there . . . or something." She managed a rather wan smile.

"It was too much for you. Altogether too much." He was frowning as he watched her. "Would you like to walk a little?"

"No." She laughed shakily. "No, thanks. I'm all right, really. I don't know why—"

"I do." Gently, he placed a hand beneath her arm. "Get into the car. Caterina should have had more sense. That—that session in there was a strain for you in every way. I do not blame the Sisters, of course— they would not understand how bad such a thing would be for you."

She realized that his car was beside them, and he was helping her into the passenger seat.

"I don't think it could have been bad for me . . ." she began, but he interrupted her.

"Naturally it was bad for you. For weeks you have been under strain, although perhaps you don't understand that. Physically and emotionally, this afternoon was simply too much for you." He glanced at her. "You could ruin your voice through such carelessness."

"But I loved doing it," she said earnestly. "And anyway, I couldn't have refused."

He said nothing, but started the engine, and they moved away along the narrow street.

"Aren't you going to wait for Caterina?" she asked involuntarily.

"No." She thought his mobile, good-humoured mouth tautened a little. "She has her own car, and besides she will probably stay with the Sisters for a while."

"Won't she wonder where I've got to?"

"She saw you leave with me."

Candy hesitated. "I know," she confessed, "that I shouldn't have done what I did this afternoon." She sensed that he was inclined to be critical of her Italian hostess's part in the afternoon's events, and although she knew it was only a temporary annoyance, caused by the fact that he had, after all, gone to a good deal of trouble recently to help with the development of her, Candy's, voice, she didn't want to be the means of causing even the smallest rift between them. She didn't understand their relationship, but it seemed to her obvious that there was something between them, and it would be dreadful if she were to be responsible for any kind of coolness between two people who had done so much to help her. "I know," she went on, "that I shouldn't really sing at all without asking you or Signor Galleo what you think. You've been so kind—you've done so much to help me. . . ."

She broke off, feeling unhappy and uncomfortable, and after a moment he spoke quietly. Actually, she thought, his voice sounded a little odd.

"I don't want you to be grateful to me, Candida—I don't want you to thank me. If I have done anything for you it is because. . . ." There was a long pause while he negotiated a dangerous roundabout. "It is because I love music," he finished rather abruptly. "And now I am particularly anxious—" He hesitated, and she glanced at him.

"Anxious?" she repeated.

"I should not tell you anything," he said rather ruefully. "It should be for Lorenzo. But I think he doesn't plan to tell you until after Christmas, and it is important that you know now so that you can prepare yourself. So that you understand how hard you must work, and how careful you should be with your voice."

Candy looked round at him with widened eyes. "What—what do you mean?" she asked.

"I mean . . ." his voice sounded intense, eager, "I mean that soon now, Candida, your career is going to begin. An opening has been arranged for you—*the* opening. In Florence, on February the seventh, there will be a performance of *Faust*. A gala performance— part of the celebrations for Martedi Grasso."

Candy felt frightened. "But I couldn't—surely you don't mean . . . Not that sort of chorus. I couldn't!"

"Couldn't you?" They were in another quiet street now, not far from Caterina's apartment, and he drew into the kerb and switched off the engine. "I am sure you could, Candida, but you are not being asked to join the chorus." Unexpectedly, he leaned across and touched her hand. "You are being asked to take the leading part—*you* will be Marguerite!"

Candy felt slightly sick. She looked out of the window at the high, ochre-tinted garden wall beside which they had come to rest, and swallowed.

"Did you say . . . Marguerite?" she asked.

And in the end Candy was forced to stop arguing. The flower-seller flatly refused to accept a *centimo* more in payment than she would normally have taken for one small bunch, and when Candy tried to insist she showed signs of becoming so violently offended that the English girl saw the necessity of giving in with a good grace and accepting what amounted to a Christmas present. Obviously the old woman was going home anyway, so it was unlikely that she was being deprived of too much—though Candy was sure she would have been just as generous if she had stood to lose a good deal.

When she finally parted the Italian woman beamed as if the transaction had delighted her. Drawing an ancient coat around her shoulders, she waved a bony hand in farewell. *"Buon natale, signorina!"*

"Buon natale. E mille grazie!"

When she got back to the apartment Candy took the mimosa to the kitchen, for Caterina to bestow in vases when she had the time, and then she went to her room realizing with something of a shock that in less than three hours' time she and Caterina were supposed to be at the Palazzo Lucca. The thought of the evening ahead made her nervous and a little uneasy, for it was not just a question of being entertained by Michele, and meeting a few of his friends. Even that, soothing as Michele's company always was, would have been a little bit alarming, but this was something altogether different. The whole of the *palazzo* was to be opened up for the occasion, and it would undoubtedly be a glittering evening. More than that, Michele's mother—Anna Landi—was to act hostess for him. Because of this

Candy's first, instinctive reaction had been to refuse the invitation, and although she had realized almost at once that this was out of the question she found it quite impossible to free herself from the obstinate shadow that hovered at the back of her mind whenever she remembered that once again she was going to have to spend an evening in the society of the woman who had taken John from her. Perhaps even in the society of John himself.

As this thought came to her she was sitting in front of her dressing-table, and she actually saw her face, framed by the heavy silver beauty of the old Venetian mirror, turn paler. If she had to see John *again* it would be dreadful. Surely Michele, tactful and kind as he invariably was, wouldn't allow. . . .

Firmly, she took herself in hand, and got up to extract from her wardrobe the dress that she had bought especially for this occasion. It was the first new evening dress she had acquired for quite some time, and she had only purchased it because she had absolutely nothing else that could possibly be considered suitable for a formal dinner at the Palazzo Lucca. It was of white silk, with here and there a touch of silvery embroidery, and its high-necked bodice and graceful, ankle-length skirt had a look of being quite separate from one another, though in actual fact they were not. She hadn't realized how well the dress suited her until shortly after six o'clock that evening, when she finally stepped into it, and even then, as she stood studying her slim reflection critically in the tall cheval mirror, she had no real idea how breathtaking she looked. She knew that her hair was behaving particularly well, and that her skin was very clear—she was quite pleased with her make-up, which certainly wasn't exaggerated, but somehow did just the right things for her lovely, luminous eyes and her soft, well-shaped mouth.

But what she just didn't know was that she was ravishingly beautiful—that in the slim, simply cut white dress she looked more like the ethereal shade of a legendary nymph than a flesh-and-blood young woman.

At half past six she went through to the *salotto*, and there she found Caterina already waiting for her. The Italian girl was looking strikingly elegant in floating apple-green velvet which suited her better than anything Candy had ever seen her wear, and her beautiful black hair was piled high on top of her head. She looked what she was—a Roman woman from one of the best families, with four thousand years of civilization in her blood. Candy was filled with enthusiastic admiration, and immediately said so.

"You're always so composed," she added a little enviously. "I wish—I wish I could be like that."

The other girl smiled at her. "I am different from you, *cara*," she said rather quietly.

The Palazzo Lucca was situated close to the Piazza del Popolo, in the part of Rome that at the time of the Renaissance had been the most fashionable area in which to live. It was a magnificently beautiful stone building, and as Candy's eyes took it in for the first time through the windscreen of Caterina's car her breath caught in her throat. It seemed to her fantastic that an edifice which looked as if it might well house a national museum, and which was certainly worthy of figuring as one of the artistic attractions of the city, should in fact be a private dwelling-place—and the dwelling, at that, of somebody she, Candy, knew quite well. Possibly Michele didn't normally put very much of the Palazzo Lucca to use, but it was, nevertheless, his house!

The whole of the narrow street in front of the Palazzo seemed to be jammed with cars, some of them already parked, some still manoeuvring to find a place, and they had to wait for nearly a minute in the middle of the road while the driver of a gleaming white Jaguar tried every way he could think of to squeeze his vehicle into a space better suited to a Mini. Eventually he gave the idea up, and as he leant forward to smile apologetically at the two girls, whom he had only just noticed, Candy saw who it was. It was some time since she had last encountered Michele's uncle, but he was too much like his nephew not to be easily recognizable.

He wound his window down. "Good evening, *signorine*! Caterina, my child, don't try to park your car. We should both have come earlier, but now the middle of the road is all that is left to us, and the middle of the road it must be." He glanced over his shoulder at the place into which he had been trying to manoeuvre himself. "On the other hand, *carina*, there is a space here just large enough for a bicycle—perhaps two bicycles. For myself I find it is of no use, but that nice little toy of yours might fit."

"*Bene*, I will try," Caterina laughed, and as the Jaguar glided off to cruise along the line of cars in search of a more suitable place she succeeded without too much difficulty in easing her own neat vehicle into the space referred to. Then she and Candy climbed out, and the English girl stood looking up at the façade of the Palazzo. Lines of tall windows that made her think vaguely of the windows at Buckingham Palace were ablaze with light, and light was flooding too from a huge central archway above which what she supposed were the arms of the di Lucca family were blazoned for the edification of the passing centuries in ponderous stone. A party of people who had just alighted from a car parked further down the street were moving under the arch, and the two girls followed them. High above their heads an enormous bronze lantern swung, and ahead of them a wide courtyard like a theatrical backdrop gave some idea of the splendours they were approaching.

The courtyard was filled with pale marble statuary and softly whispering fountains, and there were small palm trees that rustled in the night breeze. Men and women in evening dress were standing about in clusters, exchanging voluble Christmas greetings by the light of well-positioned *flambeaux*, and most of the women, Candy noticed, were protected from the slight but definite chill by expensive furs. There was the flash of jewels, too—the sort of jewels that it would undoubtedly be quite a responsibility to wear—and some of the dresses were spectacularly beautiful. On the far side of the courtyard a fan-shaped marble staircase rose to the first of a series of galleries, and as Candy slowly climbed it at Caterina's side she looked about her with the astonished fascination of a child let loose in Aladdin's cave.

And then, at the top of the steps, she received a slight shock, for here her hostess was standing and the moment of her evening to which she had looked forward with a certain amount of apprehension was upon her.

The Contessa di Lucca—otherwise known as Miss Anna Landi—was swathed from head to foot in the silky folds of a scarlet and gold sari, and she looked, Candy thought, like a lovely slender flame. Her carefully made-up face was flawlessly beautiful and she was smiling a lot, showing off her small, perfect white teeth. On one of her fingers a huge ruby glimmered and flashed as if it were alive, and there was something about her that seemed almost unreal.

She recognized Candy immediately and greeted her enthusiastically, kissing her, as she had done before, on both cheeks.

"Candida, how lovely you look! It's nice to be young. To wear white, and not appear ridiculous! But I am so happy to see you again. Caterina, *mia cara*. . . ."

And then she broke off, for just at that moment her brother-in-law, Michele's uncle, reached the top of the stairs, having apparently disposed of the Jaguar, and subtly her expression changed.

"Marco, you are late!" She was smiling at him brilliantly, as if to make up for the sudden harshness in her voice, but even the smile was a little taut. "Without Michele I should have been lost!"

"Without Michele you would always be lost, Anna." Her brother-in-law bowed over her hand, raising the vivid tips of her fingers to his lips. He stood looking at her with his head on one side, and his smile was a little strange. "You don't look lost," he remarked.

She drew her hand away from him abruptly, and gestured vaguely in Candy's direction. "I have a job for you, my friend. You are to look after this child, and see to it that she meets everybody. It is a pleasant job, yes?"

"Yes," he agreed. He turned to Candy, and a certain tension in the uneven lines of his face relaxed. "Little Signorina Wells, I am very happy at what I hear of you."

"What do you hear of me?" Candy asked, smilingly. He had put a hand beneath her elbow to propel her forward, and with a sensation of relief she left the Contessa to receive the remainder of her guests.

"I hear that your voice is becoming strong and beautiful, and soon it will be being used to delight us all."

Her lips twisted wryly. "I'm a little better than I was."

"That is not what I hear."

"What do you hear, *signore*?"

"I hear that when you sing it is a sound to enchant the nightingales. That you are to be a *prima donna* who will create history. *È vero*, I assure you."

She stood still, looking up at him. "Who told you that?"

The smile in his eyes was teasing and thoughtful at the same time. "Who has heard you sing?" he countered.

"Not many people. And nobody could have thought—"

"Ah, but they did."

They were moving on now through a series of long, high-ceilinged rooms, each one slightly more magnificent than the one before it, and suddenly, as Candy looked around her in fascinated admiration, a portrait caught her eye. It startled her so much that she almost stood still, and as he glanced round her companion laughed softly.

"So you have noticed Paolo, my distant ancestor. He is, like Michele, no?"

"Yes ... it's astonishing." They went over to study the portrait more closely, and Candy felt shaken, for the nearer she got to the painting the more difficult it was to believe that the man in dark doublet and snowy ruff who stood looking down at her from his heavy gilded frame was *not* Michele di Lucca. Without realizing it, she stood staring up at the beautifully regular features and the grave dark eyes for nearly a minute before she spoke. Then: "Who was he?" she asked.

"He was Paolo, Conte di Lucca, and he lived during the sixteenth century, when Rome was a very bad city."

"And was he bad?" Looking up at the thoughtful eyes and the humorous mouth, she found it very difficult to believe.

"No, he was not. He was a fighter, but he fought for the return of honour and order and justice when this city had forgotten that such ideals existed."

"And did he succeed—I mean, did he do anything to improve things?"

The descendant of Paolo di Lucca shrugged, and glanced up at his forebear with a trace of rueful affection. "Perhaps not. But at least he himself remained incorruptible." Almost under his breath he added: "And that is not always easy. That can require more courage than anything!"

Something in his voice made Candy look round at him with curiosity, but he had taken her arm again, and was urging her back into the thickening crowd of guests.

It was not long after that that she caught sight of John Ryland. She was in the process of being whisked from group to glittering group, and was beginning to feel slightly dizzy and to wish that Marco di Lucca would stop taking his responsibility for her entertainment quite so seriously. He seemed to think it was his duty to make sure that she was introduced to as large a proportion of Roman society as was possible in the time, and the bewildering variety of faces, coupled with the noise and laughter all around her, was giving her a headache. Everyone seemed to smile on her benevolently—possibly some of the women were less benevolent than the men, but even they were reasonably affable— and she supposed she ought to be enjoying herself tremendously, but the nagging feeling that something was missing, that she couldn't possibly be enjoying herself completely, which had been present with her ever since John ceased to be part of her life was somehow stronger than ever.

And then she saw him. He was with the Contessa di Lucca, and they were moving towards her—in fact, almost before she knew it they were right beside her. She had become separated, temporarily, from the Contessa's brother-in-law, who had glimpsed an old friend on the other side of the room, and having also just succeeded in throwing off the persistent attentions of one of the dozens of young Romans for whom she seemed to have the fascination of a magnet she was, at that moment, without any means of escape. The Contessa bore down on her.

"Candida, *carissima*! Does Marco not look after you, the bad one?"

"He's been looking after me very well," Candy assured her hastily, and then she found herself looking at John. He glanced at her sheepishly, and then away, but she suddenly realized that she herself had no feeling of confusion. She didn't really feel anything at all, except that as she studied his face with the calm of a strange new detachment it struck her for the first time that, as a face, it contained remarkably little in the way of character. Although she had never realized it before, it was an empty face—empty and weak. She suddenly felt very clear-headed and cool.

"Well, enjoy yourself!" Extending a slim forefinger, the Contessa patted her cheek. "At your age, and looking as you do, it should not be difficult!" All at once she glanced round, and a warmer smile touched her lips. "And here is someone else to take charge of you."

Candy looked round, and with a small start she realized that Michele had joined them. He had come up so quietly that she hadn't noticed him, but now she saw he was looking at her—watching her with a queer bright intensity. His eyes were rather serious, yet there was a half smile on his lips. His gaze seemed to draw her own, and because she couldn't help it she found herself staring into his soft dark eyes as if something in their depths had laid a spell on her. A little shiver ran through her, and all at once she began to feel the thudding of her own heart.

And then she looked away, half conscious of a sudden interested alertness in the face of the Conte's mother, and knew that now she really did feel dizzy. The room was revolving around her—the world was turning upside down—and it was all because her eyes had met the eyes of Michele di Lucca. Because while they were gazing at one another she had entered another world, and she needed time to readjust.

CHAPTER EIGHT

AFTER those few short moments during which something strange and vital had seemed to flash between them, Michele reverted to treating Candy with his usual blend of gentleness and reserve, and in fact it seemed to her that he was slightly more reserved than usual. He apologized for not being on hand to greet her when she arrived, and told her she looked 'most charming', but there was a formality about his every word that made her feel he was treating her like a stranger. She was bewildered, and after a time a sort of dull chill seemed to settle over her. For weeks she had taken his kindness, his attentiveness, for granted.... Now, suddenly, it was important that he should notice her—so important that once, as he turned away from her to speak to somebody else, she actually felt the prickle of moisture behind her eyelids—and just as suddenly he had evidently decided to relegate her to a lower place in his scheme of things. She didn't feel resentful, for she told herself that after all there was no reason why he should pay her so much attention—and tonight he was more than fully occupied with his brilliant concourse of guests—but no matter how hard she tried to reason with herself the strange chill persisted.

And then she saw him with Caterina, laughing and talking, looking relaxed for the first time that evening, and the chill intensified as she remembered something she had forgotten . . . the fact that, quite obviously, he was Caterina's property, and if he were going to show a particular interest in anyone it would be her.

After a time Marco di Lucca rejoined her, full of apologies for his neglect, and at the same time expressing the certainty that she wouldn't have had time to notice his absence.

"I am sure you have not been alone," he told her. "Once I looked, and. . . ." An expressive gesture. "There was nothing to see but the top of your head. You were surrounded!"

"People are . . . friendly," Candy said abstractedly and a little foolishly, and the Italian put his head on one side and regarded her thoughtfully for a moment or two.

"You are tired?" he asked.

"No—no, of course not." She smiled brightly. "It's all so fascinating and bewildering, though. I feel a little bit lost."

"Well, I will not leave you again." He smiled back at her with paternal benevolence, and lightly put an arm about her shoulders. "Come and have some supper."

The buffet supper, set out on long tables in the *palazzo*'s sumptuous *sala da pranzo*, was bewilderingly lavish and colourful. If Candy had been feeling hungry she might have been able to do reasonable justice to the bewildering array of cold meats and pastry confections, and the mountains of gleaming fruit, but as it was all she could face was a microscopic portion of chicken, followed by fruit salad and black coffee. She had already had a glass of sherry, and she firmly refused anything further in the nature of alcoholic refreshment.

Nothing her companion could say had any power to alter her decision, but he himself seemed to place no such limitations on his intake.

It was some time before Candy began to realize that Marco was drinking too much, and even then she didn't think nearly as much of it as she might have done in different circumstances. In this strange, glittering, bewildering world of Roman 'high society' people obviously didn't behave at any time as they might have been expected to behave back in her mother-in-law's village of Great Mincham, and even in that model English parish itself a certain amount of over-indulgence was by no means uncommon on Christmas Eve. For some time she had been becoming convinced that Marco di Lucca was anything but a happy man, and she supposed any excuse to drown his sorrows would be too big a temptation to resist. In any case, it didn't seem to her that the effects showed particularly, and after supper she was still grateful for his protection against the bewildering overtures of his fellow-countrymen. In one of the long rooms a few couples were dancing, rather lethargically, to music provided by a pianist and a couple of violinists, and after a time Marco asked Candy if she would like to join them. She didn't really want to dance —in fact, she had the beginnings of a violent headache, and was thinking longingly of the moment when she would be able to get away—but her host's uncle seemed to feel strongly that she ought to, and rather than argue with him she allowed herself to be led out to join the twenty or thirty young Italians moving in a desultory fashion round the floor.

As it turned out, Marco di Lucca was not by any

means a brilliant dancer, and as he was also becoming increasingly abstracted she didn't find the exercise very entertaining. When the music stopped he passed a hand across his forehead as if he was feeling the effects of unaccustomed exertion, and to Candy's profound relief he suggested that they should sit down.

"I am not a good companion, little one." His voice had just a suspicion of unsteadiness about it. "I shall bore you."

"You don't bore me at all." She sat down beside him, smiling. "You've been terribly nice to me. But I do think perhaps I'm boring you. Shall I go and find Caterina?"

He shook his head. "Stay with me ... stay with me. Michele asked me to keep—keep an eye on you, as you say in England, and, *ecco*, I am doing so." He looked across the room, and Candy saw that he was watching Michele's mother, still moving among the guests like a graceful, slender flame.

"Michele asked you to keep an eye on me?" She felt a burning curiosity to know what Michele had said.

"Yes." He turned to stare at her—a strange, penetrating, appraising stare that seemed to explore her soul. "My nephew's instructions were precise. You are a rare prize, and are to be guarded."

"Why am I to be guarded?" She tried to speak lightly, but her heart was beating fast.

Marco di Lucca's expression changed. He looked away from her, and shrugged. "I told you ... you are a great hope of the musical world, a *prima donna* of the future." His eyes were once again on the brilliant figure of his sister-in-law, and Candy could tell that she herself had only half his attention, but something made her go on probing. With a faint flush in her cheeks she asked:

"Does—does Michele . . . does the Conte really think I'm good?"

The Italian turned to look at her again. Quite suddenly his good-humoured face had become old and world-weary. "You want very much to know?"

The colour deepened a little, but she said, calmly: "Yes, of course."

"For Michele you are a miracle. A beautiful talent . . . a beautiful talent that he can work upon, and then present to the world as a gift."

"Oh!" She swallowed.

"You don't wish to be a gift to the world?"

"I'm just not a beautiful talent."

"My nephew thinks you are. You can give his life a meaning. In later years, when you remember that, it will be a good feeling."

"I can—what do you mean?" Feeling oddly shaken, she stared at the man beside her as if he had temporarily taken leave of his senses. "There's so much in his life. He has everything. . . ." Caterina Marchetti to begin with, she wanted to add.

"You think a man has everything when he wakes every morning to face an almost intolerable burden?"

There was silence for a moment. As she repeated the words, Candy's voice sounded rather strange. "An intolerable burden?"

"You didn't know?" Several seconds ticked away while the Italian studied her face. Then his lips twisted wryly. "No, you didn't know."

"I don't understand."

"There is no need for you to understand. Forget what I said. It doesn't concern you."

Candy's eyes searched his face. Her own looked small and pale and troubled. "Please. . . . I'd like to know what you meant."

He leant towards her. "Listen to me, Candy." On his lips, her name sounded as if it were spelt 'Kendy'. "I'm a funny person. Sometimes I don't talk at all. You have noticed, uh? And sometimes I talk too much. I say things that don't mean anything—anything at all. What I said just now meant nothing."

She was silent, her eyes still troubled, and he reached out and patted her hand. "Come, *cara* . . . smile! It's Christmas Eve."

She knew she couldn't press him any further. If he hadn't intended to say what he had said then it would be very wrong of her to try and insist that he should enlarge upon it. But for the rest of the evening the extraordinary words nagged at her like a dull toothache. '*He wakes every morning to face an intolerable burden. An intolerable burden. . . .*'

In some countries a party such as the one that filled the Palazzo di Lucca with colour and movement that evening would have been expected to go on into the early hours of Christmas morning. But this was Italy, and punctually at a quarter to eleven everyone started to disperse in order to make their way to midnight Mass. Once again the marble staircase leading down to the courtyard glowed with the vivid hues of multi-coloured evening dresses, and from the street outside came the sound of ringing laughter and the slamming of car doors.

Candy stood on the stairs under the bright, cool, distant stars and looked around for Caterina. She hadn't seen her for some time, and for that matter she hadn't seen Michele, either. Apart from Marco di Lucca and his dazzling sister-in-law—who had paused once, in passing, to pat her cheek and express the hope that she was having a wonderful time—she hadn't seen anyone she really knew for hours, and she felt tired and a little lost. She had said good-night to Marco, thanking him for his kindness and telling him she was going to look for Caterina, but now she was beginning to wonder whether she ought to try and find him again, for the building was emptying quite rapidly, and she could see no sign of the Italian girl anywhere.

And then, all at once, she did see her. Caterina was descending the stairs very slowly, and her dark head was thrown back so that she could look up into the face of the man beside her. The man was Michele, and they were deep in a conversation so absorbing that they didn't notice Candy until they had very nearly walked past her.

And then she saw Michele's dark eyes suddenly come to rest upon her, and he said something to the girl at his side. Caterina looked round, and then she moved quickly over to the English girl.

"I was looking for you, *cara*." Her eyes were faintly conscience-stricken. "I am going to church with Michele. Signor Marco will drive you home—or to Mass first, if you would like that."

"Oh!" Candy had an awful feeling that she sounded as flat as she felt, and she made a desperate effort to alter the impression. "It's been a wonderful evening, hasn't it?"

"Yes, wonderful." The other girl looked at her seriously. "You are all right, Candida?"

"Of course. I've been having a marvellous time. I'll see you in the morning."

"Yes. Well. . . . Good-night, *cara*."

Just for a moment, over Caterina's head, Candy's eyes met the dark, inscrutable eyes of Michele. He didn't smile, or say a word, and a second later he and Caterina were moving on down the stairway into the haunted shadows of the courtyard.

For about a minute after they had disappeared from sight Candy stood exactly where they had left her, one hand on the broad marble balustrade, the other hanging a little limply by her side. Then, behind her, she heard the voice of Marco di Lucca.

"Don't look so sad, Candy."

Startled, she swung round, and with a barely noticeable gesture brushed something bright from the corner of one eye.

"Do I look sad? I'm not." And she smiled brightly up at him.

"*Bene.* Now, do I take you home, or do I take you to church? I know you are not Catholic, but it is Christmas. And it might be interesting for you to see the Mass. Especially as everyone else is going."

She hesitated. "Will you be going to Mass? I mean," a little ruefully, "will you be going even if you have to take me home first?"

"Certainly I shall go. I am a sinner of incredible

blackness, Candy, but I was very nicely brought up, and still, sometimes, I go to Mass to be whitened a little."

"Then, if you don't mind taking me with you, I'd like to go too."

The church they were going to was not far away, but there was a lot of traffic in the streets, and their progress was soon reduced to a crawl. Everywhere in Rome people seemed to be leaving parties or closing the doors of their houses behind them and pouring into the churches, and as their vehicles jammed the roads and sometimes even the pavements, and every so often there were bursts of furious honking from drivers who felt they had been held up long enough, but on the whole there was a kind of tangible good humour in the air, keen, joyous excitement, and Candy was suddenly conscious of a feeling of exhilaration. Once, as they waited, locked in an apparently immovable jam, a man jumped out of his car to run across the road and shake the hand of another driver. He held everyone up for at least two minutes longer than was strictly necessary before he finally hurried back and climbed behind his own steering-wheel again, but his light-hearted pleasure in the evidently unexpected encounter with a friend was so infectious that nobody seemed to mind in the least.

And then, moving a little faster than the cars in the lane on their left, they drew abreast of a gleaming white Fiat, and it didn't take Candy more than a second to recognize the occupants. Something of the brightness of the scene around her seemed to become dim, and she turned her eyes away from the sports car and its driver to stare into a lighted display window on the other side of the road. Michele was concentrating on the road ahead, but Caterina had her face turned towards him, and it was easy to see that she was gazing at him with a sort of eager intensity. Without wanting to go too deeply into her own reasons, Candy just didn't want to watch them.

She didn't know that Marco had been watching both the white car and her own face, and she was surprised when he suddenly said: "In a moment we shall lose them."

"I should have thought they would have been further ahead of us," she said lightly.

"Perhaps they have just been unlucky. With the traffic." He paused, and she had an uncomfortable feeling that he was looking at her. Then he said: "Candy, I should not like you to feel that you have been unlucky in Rome."

She turned her head. "Unlucky?" she repeated.

He gestured towards the sports car, now drawing quite rapidly away from them. "Don't think about him," he said briefly.

There was silence for nearly a minute, and when she spoke her voice was husky. "I don't think about him—really. That is," truthfully, "I didn't. Until. . . ."

"Until to-night? I know, *cara*. I saw the moment when it came into your eyes. Only this morning he was merely someone kind . . . a friend, yes? And to-night he is so much more."

She looked away sharply, feeling startled and bewildered. It had all been so sudden. She herself had barely had time yet to understand what was happening to her. So how could Marco . . . how could he have guessed?

"You must not be upset." He was speaking gently, staring straight in front of him. "It is not a thing to be ashamed of, falling in love. But one can be badly hurt by it. One can be hurt so badly that one wishes only to die. You think that is too dramatic—"

"No," she said quickly, "I don't."

"Then. . . . Little one, I wish only to warn you. You are just beginning to fall in love with Michele. Put him out of your mind now. Put him out of your heart."

Somewhere inside her a conventional instinct was urging her to utter some sort of denial—to refuse to discuss it, at least. But the words wouldn't come, and after a long silence all she said was :

"He's going to marry Caterina, isn't he?"

She knew that Marco di Lucca looked at her and sighed rather heavily. Then he said something beneath his breath, in Italian.

"Perhaps," he conceded.

"Then—"

"Listen, little one, there is one thing you have to do. You have to go ahead with your music. You have to sing in this opera, and you have to be successful."

She swallowed. The idea of going through with it all —of endless rehearsals for *Faust*, with Michele beside her all the time, directing and advising, made her throat feel dry. "I'm really not good enough," she said flatly.

"Lorenzo Galleo *knows* you are good enough." He spoke gently. "You must do this, Candy. You must not give up because of Michele. You must not give up for any reason. If you are unhappy now then it is now that you should dedicate yourself to work. And you will not always be unhappy."

They had reached the church now, and he drew into the kerb, behind a lot of other vehicles. Somewhere ahead of them in the line was Michele's Fiat, and as Candy got out of the car a slim figure detached itself from the crowd of humanity still pouring into the church and hurried towards her. It was Caterina, and she was holding an insubstantial black lace scarf, which she pressed into Candy's hand.

"Put it on your head," she whispered. "I waited—I remembered that you would not have one with you."

And then she slipped away again. Looking after her, Candy saw Michele's dark brown head follow hers through the lighted doorway and into the church.

Standing and kneeling through the long, colourful ceremony of the Mass, her nose assailed by incense, her eyes dazzled by the glow of hundreds of candles, Candy's thoughts were for most of the time in a turmoil. She was profoundly grateful for the press of humanity around her, for their happy, rustling, murmuring presence gave her a feeling of being part of something outside herself which helped to ease, a little, the aching unhappiness at the centre of her being. The throbbing organ seemed to soothe her bruised and bewildered spirit, too, and very gradually the blackness of the depression hanging over her lightened just a little. But nothing seemed to clear the despairing confusion in her mind, and it wasn't until the final blessing had been given, and above the soaring strains of *Adeste Fideles* the Christmas bells were starting to peal out across the city, that the mists clinging about her thinking powers began to evaporate.

And then, quite suddenly, she knew that Marco di

Lucca was right. She must go on with her singing career. Here, in Rome, with Michele or without him, she must work to justify the confidence that had been placed in her. She must take the part of Marguerite and she must do her best to make a success of it.

But only she herself, and perhaps Marco, would ever know how much it was going to cost her.

CHAPTER NINE

THE next few weeks were the most exhausting and bewildering that Candy had ever experienced. She seemed to work day and night, pausing only for rest, for short walks through the wintry city, for increasingly light meals—increasingly light only because she felt less and less capable of facing food. Her health was undoubtedly suffering, as everyone around her noticed with genuine concern. But they attributed it all to tension and excitement and the strain of all the hard, gruelling work she was putting in—work that was absolutely essential if she was to stand any chance of meeting the challenge of the seventh of February with any success. They saw with approval that she was really keen to achieve that success, and for the most part they imagined she thought of very little else.

In actual fact she was profoundly thankful for the fact that the ordeal ahead of her—and she couldn't think of it as anything but an ordeal—left her with so little time to think. She not only had to learn and perfect her presentation of a series of difficult and demanding arias, but for the first time in her life—if she were to discount the part of a small angel, once allocated to her in a school Nativity Play—her acting ability was to be put to the test in public. At first, on top of all the effort and concentration called for by the musical side, it had all seemed far too much for her to attempt to tackle with success, but Signor Galleo had been bracing on the subject. Theatrical ability, he remarked, came naturally to women, and he had no reason to believe that Candy was any exception. He did, however, arrange for a certain amount of drama coaching to be added to her curriculum, and within a short time the idea of impersonating another human being on a stage began to hold fewer terrors for her. Signor Galleo was actually far more pleased than he would have been prepared to admit with the rapidity of her progress in every respect, and his confidence in her increased every day.

Michele was unfailingly kind and unfailingly helpful, and in spite of everything during the hours when she was with him she was almost happy. Sometimes she would be singing and he would be accompanying her, sometimes he would be helping her to learn the complicated French libretto—yet another hurdle to be crossed—and sometimes they would simply be talking over a break for coffee and sandwiches, but whenever she was with him she felt that in a curious way they were completely and utterly in sympathy with one another, and while they were together the uncomfortable memory of his uncle's words—even the shadow of Caterina, who didn't often take part in these sessions— seemed obliterated as if nothing of the sort had ever been.

Very early in January she met Giulio Preti, the Italian tenor who was to sing opposite her in Florence, together with the rest of the cast, and thereafter she had to take part in frequent joint rehearsals. Everyone was friendly and helpful, and although Giulio was decidedly overweight and anything but good-looking he was a very competent singer whose support on stage was obviously going to be invaluable to her. Gradually, very gradually, she began to feel more at home in the part, less appalled by the vastness of the whole undertaking.

But the strain grew progressively greater, and by the evening of February first, as she returned alone to Caterina's flat after a lengthy session with Signor Galleo, she knew she felt decidedly odd. She had been singing for more than five hours with very little in the way of rest, and she hadn't bothered to eat much that day, either. The following morning they were all due to leave for Florence, and she found herself wondering suddenly just how she was going to face it all.

Slowly, she made her way up in the lift, and let herself into Caterina's flat. Then she closed the front door behind her and leant against it. And instantly a voice spoke to her.

"So very tired, Candida?"

It was Michele. She had closed her eyes, but now she opened them quickly, and stood up straight. "Not really tired," she lied valiantly. "I'll be quite all right after a good night's sleep."

"Are you sure?" He was frowning a little.

"Absolutely sure."

He helped her out of her coat, and guided her through into Caterina's sitting-room as if she were an exhausted child. Caterina didn't seem to be anywhere about.

"You are ready to leave for Florence in the morning?"

"Yes." With a trace of anxiety she added: "You're going to join us at the station, aren't you?"

"No, Candida. That's one of the reasons why I came to see you to-night. I shall not be going to Florence with you."

Afterwards she could only hope that the dismay she felt hadn't shown too clearly in her face. "You aren't coming?" she repeated a little stupidly.

"No. I have to go abroad—to Switzerland. It is ... unexpected business. I must go. I am sorry, because I wanted to help you as much as I could, but I am sure you will be all right without me."

She wanted to say that of course she wouldn't be all right, that she would be lost without him. But all she actually said was : "I hope you have a good journey. Do you leave to-morrow?"

"The following day. But to-morrow I shall have many things to do. I may not have time to see you off at the station."

"Oh!" She made a brave attempt to smile. "Well, I'll do my best not to let you down. You've been such a wonderful help to me."

"I am glad." Abruptly, he stood up. "I came only to say good-bye ... *arrivederci*. You are tired to-night, and there is no need to give you more advice now. We have been over everything, and besides you will have with you people much better qualified than I am to help you."

At the door of the flat she gave him her hand, and he held it for several seconds in a light but remarkably comforting clasp that she felt for a long time afterwards. A little uncertainly, she said :

"You will be in Florence for the performance ... won't you?"

He looked down at her, and his brown eyes took on a strange, unreadable expression.

"Of course, Candida, I shall be there to support you. And now, good-night . . . and good-bye until we meet again."

And then he turned and left her. A moment or two later she heard the clash of the lift doors, and knew that he had really gone.

The next morning it was raining hard, and she awoke with the beginnings of a headache, and the knowledge that she didn't feel in the least like setting out for Florence. But there was no possibility of avoiding what had been planned for her, and punctually at half past nine, as they had been instructed, she and Caterina arrived at Rome's central railway station. Caterina was insisting on going with her to Florence, and she was grateful, for she had grown really fond of the Italian girl. Somehow, she couldn't feel resentful of whatever relationship it was that existed between her and Michele. Not, as she constantly reminded herself, that she had any right to feel resentful, anyway.

At the station they were met by Lorenzo Galleo and Giulio Preti, both very alert and cheerful despite the damp greyness of the morning, and one by one the rest of the cast arrived to join them. Laughing and chattering in English and Italian, they all climbed aboard the long, streamlined, north-bound train, and precisely at ten o'clock they began to draw slowly out of Rome.

Candy, looking very English and very attractive in a misty turquoise woollen suit, attracted a good many interested glances from her travelling companions, both male and female, but she didn't feel at all in the mood for conversation, and for most of the time she buried herself in an absorbing book which Michele had thought might be of use to her. Michele. . . .

Time and again she put the book downward, staring through the rain-streaked window at an endless vista of dimly-seen grey olive slopes and distant hills, wondered why Michele couldn't have been with her. Whatever the business was that was taking him to Switzerland, it must be important, for she was sure he hadn't wanted to let her down. And besides, if he had come to Florence he could have been with Caterina. . . .

They reached the city of Dante and the Medici during the afternoon. It was raining harder than it had been in Rome, and it was also a good deal colder. Candy, who felt tired and stiff, was grateful for the smooth efficiency with which she and her fellows were whisked from the station to their hotel, and still more grateful for the fact that she was immediately left alone to rest. Only a few months earlier the last thing she would have wanted to do on arrival in Florence was lie down and have a nap, but these days, outside working hours, she was almost always tired.

The hotel they had all been taken to was a comfortable middle-grade establishment, and her room was small but well furnished. After taking one look through the wide plate-glass windows at the rain-soaked rooftops of Florence she curled up on the bed with her book, and almost immediately fell asleep.

She was awakened about an hour later by the sound of the telephone ringing close beside her. The room was almost in darkness, and as she struggled into a sitting position she reached first for the receiver and then for the light switch.

At the other end of the telephone line a man's voice spoke, rather uncertainly.

"Is that Candy?"

"Yes." Who *did* that voice belong to?

"It's me . . . John."

"John?" There was a pause, and then realization hit her. "Oh!"

"Candy, I'm in Florence. Just a couple of blocks away from you, as a matter of fact." He waited, but there was no answer. "Candy?"

"Yes. Yes, I'm here."

"Did you hear what I said? It's ridiculous, when I'm within walking distance of your hotel, but this line doesn't seem too good."

"I can hear you very well, John." Her voice had never sounded calmer.

"Good. Listen, Candy, I want to see you. I'm dying to see you." Another short pause. "Will you have dinner with me to-night?"

She sighed, but so softly that he didn't hear. "Haven't you got a date with the Contessa di Lucca?"

She heard him say something violent under his breath. "No! Anna's in Rome, and I shan't be seeing her again. Candy, I've a lot to explain—"

She interrupted him. "No, you haven't. You haven't got anything to explain. I don't know anything about your . . . your relationship with the Contessa, but that doesn't matter, because it's nothing to do with me."

"Don't be absurd!" The voice she had once thought so shatteringly attractive sounded irritated. "Darling,

I've made a fool of myself, I know that, but—hang it all, she is one of the most beautiful women in the world! When I met her I was hypnotized. Any man would have been the same. But it's over now, and—Candy, are you there?"

"Yes. But, John—"

"Well, listen to me, will you? I love you, Candy. I suppose I always have done, but it took this little—episode to get it sorted out in my mind." There was a moment's hesitation, and when he went on his tone was subtly confident. "Look, we can't talk over the phone. I'll pick you up at half past seven, and we'll go out and discover Florence. It'll be an evening to remember!"

"You go out and discover Florence, John, and I hope you do have an evening to remember." Her voice was cool and even. "But I'm tired to-night, and I've got a good deal of work ahead of me. Thanks for asking, but I'd rather not. And I don't think we have anything to talk about." She waited a moment, and then said quietly: "Good-night, John."

She lowered the receiver to its rest, and then a few seconds later picked it up again to speak to the hotel switchboard.

"I'm sorry to be a nuisance," she heard herself saying, "but I'd really rather not have any more calls put through to me to-night. Yes, room three hundred and ninety-one."

She hung up again, and leant back against the bed's padded headboard. Well, she had settled that. He might try to get in touch with her in other ways, he might ring her in the morning, but she would just go on finding means of avoiding him until, finally, the message penetrated. He probably wouldn't persevere very long, in any case.

The call had certainly been a bit of a shock, and she knew that if she were to be honest with herself she would have to admit that her vanity had been gratified. She wouldn't have been a normal woman if she had not derived some satisfaction from the knowledge that the man whom she had once imagined herself desperately in love with, and who had been stolen from under her nose by the fantastic Anna Landi, had now come rushing back to throw himself, metaphorically speaking, at her feet. Admittedly, there had been little enough in the way of humility about his attitude on the telephone, but then, as she realized now, humility in the ordinary sense just wasn't possible with John.

She sighed, and was conscious of a feeling of peace. John was out of her system once and for all—he no longer had any hold over her. And she knew that whatever it was that she had felt for him it had not been love.

For the next four days Candy and the rest of the cast worked almost non-stop. Dividing their time between the Hotel Michelangelo—where their expenses were being met by the rather obscure fund which had financed the whole enterprise—and the imposing baroque theatre in which their performance was to be staged they saw about as little as it was possible to see of the city on the Arno, but Candy at least felt no urge whatsoever to engage in sightseeing activities, and everybody else seemed to have been familiar with Florence since early childhood.

On the morning of Martedì Grasso—the Italian name

for Shrove Tuesday—Candy awoke to find that the rain which had been falling steadily ever since the morning of her departure from Rome had disappeared at last, and the city was bathed in the glow of a golden sunrise. There wasn't a cloud to be seen anywhere, and when, on impulse, she flung her bedroom window open and leant out to look down into the glistening street she was greeted, unaccountably, by the drifting scent of invisible mimosa. Drawing a deep breath, she closed her eyes, and the strain and weariness and tension that she had lived with, day by day, for weeks, seemed to recede a little.

But it didn't recede for long, and by the time she had eaten a hurried breakfast in her room and had gone down to the Company's private sitting-room to meet Lorenzo Galleo she was as taut and keyed up as a well-tuned violin string. The Italian's eyes narrowed a little as he looked at her, and he came to meet her, taking both her hands in his.

"Candida. . . ." He smiled at her. "My child, you must relax."

She smiled back at him, a little helplessly. "I know, but I can't."

"Sit down." Watching her as she obeyed him, his brows contracted a little. "You know, it is perfectly natural that you should be very tense, very nervous just now. And because you have had to work so very hard to prepare yourself for this performance in such a short time it is also natural that you should be tired. But you are more than tense, more than nervous, more than tired." He laughed a little, shaking his head at her. "Almost, you make me feel that I should call a doctor, and ask him to tell me if you are well enough to go ahead!"

"Oh, but that's ridiculous ... I'm quite all right. I'm fine!"

For a moment or two he was silent, staring at her. And then, almost imperceptibly, he shrugged. *"Benissimo!* And now, what would you like to do to-day?"

"Do...? Well, I suppose I'll be—rehearsing, won't I?"

"Not to-day. You have worked very hard, without rest and without complaining, but you have worked enough. I do not think that another rehearsal would help your performance to-night at all."

"I am flattered. Then you remember, of course, that I told you hard work would be necessary."

"I've never forgotten it."

"That I realize." Once again he smiled his wide, paternal smile. "But if I had known that you were going to be such a good pupil I would also have told you that it is possible to work too much as well as too little. It is good to be a fine singer," teasingly, "but not if one has no strength left with which to sing!"

"I have plenty of strength, *signore.* For singing."

"Well, well, that's good." He hesitated, feeling oddly unsure of himself. "I told you also that you must lose yourself in your music. But, you know, I did not really mean that you should lose yourself completely, so completely. When you came to me one could see that you were unhappy. Then, I thought, you became happier. Now ... now you are unhappy again."

She looked away from him, and out of the window at the sunny morning. "I've just been getting a bit nervous," she said after a pause. "I'll be all right by to-morrow."

Lorenzo Galleo sighed, and decided that no good could come of further probing at the moment. He stood up. "Very well. Now, what would you say to a little walk in the sunshine?"

She shook her head. "No, I don't think.... Oh, I'm sorry. I'm being terribly difficult."

"But," a little desperately, "I must do something."

"Then do whatever you would like to do—provided it is not too tiring, of course! But no more work until the curtain rises to-night. You understand me?"

"I feel much better when I'm working," she pleaded. "I don't get so ... so edgy."

"I know, I know." Sitting down beside her, he studied her with an anxiety that he tried to keep out of his eyes. When he had taken her on, three months earlier, as totally untried material, he had thought it important to explain to her, as he did to all his pupils, that the road ahead would be anything but an easy one. Hard work and a sense of dedication, he had told her, were indispensable if she were to achieve even the smallest measure of success. But he hadn't really expected her to take him so seriously. She had worked as he had never known a pupil work before, and although, recognizing the real value of her developing talent, he had been delighted by her single-mindedness it hadn't been long before he had also begun to be afraid that she might overdo it. She was a sensitive, emotional sort of girl, and physically rather fragile. In such a case, too much dedication could be even more dangerous than too little.

"Do you remember, Candida," he asked her now, "what I told you when you first came to me?"

"Yes, *signore*. Every word."

"To-day you have a right to be difficult. Would you —perhaps you would just like to be left alone?"

"Oh, *please*!" She looked up at him gratefully.

"Then I will leave you. But—" He stood still. "Candida, there is one thing that I wanted to ask you."

"What is it, *signore*?"

"Are you happy about appearing to-night? Or do you feel that you have been hurried into this . . . that it is too soon, that you are not ready to appear in public?"

"What do you think?" she asked quietly.

"I know that you are ready, but I wish to be sure that you will not do this against your will."

"It won't be against my will. I want to go ahead, and I want to be successful." And something inside her added : "Because there is nothing else in life."

Candy spent the rest of the day trying to rest. By tacit consent everybody seemed to leave her alone, and she spent a good deal of the time in her room, reading— the only occupation that enabled her to keep still at all. As the day wore on she grew more and more keyed up, and was annoyed with herself, for she knew it wasn't only the thought of the performance looming ahead of her that was throwing her off balance. Something was missing—or rather somebody—and she didn't merely wish he were with her; without him she felt as lost as a dinghy in the middle of the Pacific Ocean.

John Ryland had tried to telephone her twice, but as on both occasions she had put the receiver down without hesitation he seemed to have given up. Once, apparently, he had turned up in person and asked for her at the reception desk, but she had flatly refused to see him, and now she was hoping against hope that he really understood. She couldn't have cared less whether he resumed his violent interest in the beautiful Anna, or, for that matter, removed himself to a monastery, but the idea of having to speak to him nauseated her. She realized, now, that her feelings for him had been essentially childish, the result, mainly, of a desperate urge to cling to something...anything. All at once, with astonishing clarity, she saw all the things in him that were least attractive...his weakness, his selfishness, his conceit. But at the same time she knew that if she had really loved him—if between them there had been that mysterious bond of magnetism which defies all explanation—no fault of which the human character was capable would have made any difference. She hadn't loved him, and she knew she was very lucky to have escaped the disaster that might have overtaken her if his own ideas where she was concerned had clarified themselves a little earlier. She felt like someone who has only just discovered how close they have been to the edge of a precipice. She might have been married to him!

As for his own feelings for herself, she had very little doubt that they would evaporate soon enough. In his world there were plenty of Anna Landis. He wouldn't go without consolation for long.

At five o'clock an excellent English-style tea was brought to her room, accompanied by a message of good wishes from the hotel manager. She sent the

manager a note of thanks and poured herself a cup of
tea, but left the cakes and sandwiches untouched, rather
wishing she didn't have to look at them. There had still
been no message of any kind from Michele, and she was
fighting against a kind of rising panic.

What, she wondered, would she do if he didn't come?
She knew she was probably crazy to allow herself to
depend on him in any way whatsoever—when, as he had
shown so clearly on Christmas night, Caterina was the
only person in the world who really meant anything to
him—but she couldn't help it. If only, just this once,
he could be there to give her courage. . . . Afterwards,
she would have to fight her battles alone, for she knew
she must stop seeing him, but she didn't want to
think about that now. Not yet.

It occurred to her that if Michele didn't come
Caterina probably wouldn't come either. She really
was going to be alone.

Soon after five a cable was delivered to her, and
even before she opened it she knew it was from Sue
and Paul.

'Best possible luck, darling. Everyone thrilled to bits.'
She read the words several times before returning them
to their envelope, and she thought briefly that it was
nice to know there was still someone in the world who
took a personal interest in her.

Immediately after that Lorenzo Galleo telephoned
through to her room. His voice with its heavy accent
was cheerful and reassuring, and as he suggested to
her that possibly they ought soon to be thinking of
setting out for the theatre she didn't feel nearly as
panicky as she had expected to feel. She felt rather flat,

and also rather cold inside, but on the whole she was conscious of a strange new sense of detachment.

They reached the theatre soon after six, and as she sat in her dressing-room with several of the other girls involved in the production fussing around her sympathetically she wondered for a moment if she could be dreaming. This couldn't be her, Candy Wells. It didn't make sense. She didn't feel excited, she couldn't honestly have said that she was nervous—everything was completely unreal.

The performance was scheduled to begin at half past seven, and by seven o'clock she was fully dressed, and as near to being ready as she was likely to be. Giulio Preti came and talked to her for a few minutes, but once they had gone over the various musical technicalities that it was important they should go into their conversation more or less dried up, and he disappeared again.

Then another cable was delivered to her. Almost without thinking, she opened it slowly, and it wasn't until the slip of cream-coloured paper was spread in front of her that the fingers holding it started to tremble, and the blood pounded wildly in her veins. It was from Michele. . . . And it had been sent from Switzerland.

'*I cannot be with you.* . . .' The lines blurred in front of her eyes. '*Sing as you have never sung. God bless you. Michele.*'

Her hand dropped, and the cable fluttered to the floor. She was thankful that she was alone. He couldn't come . . . he didn't say he was sorry. But he did say: 'God bless you !'

She sat down slowly on the chair in front of her

dressing-table, and stared unseeingly at her own unreal, carefully made-up reflection.

And at that moment there was a sudden outburst of raised voices in the passageway outside the door. At first she scarcely noticed it, but it was followed almost immediately by a violent shaking of the door itself. Somebody was evidently trying to turn the handle, and was being forcibly prevented from obtaining entry. Still she sat gazing into the mirror, unable somehow to summon up the interest or even the enegry to find out what was going on, but a few seconds later persistence was rewarded, and the door swung open. On the threshold stood the Contessa di Lucca.

She was wearing a magnificent sable coat, and from head to toe she was as perfectly turned out as she almost invariably seemed to be, but underneath its flawless make-up her beautiful face looked pale, and her eyes were wide and strained. Behind her stood Lorenzo Galleo, his face almost as taut as her own.

"This . . . man would not let me come in!" The famous beauty gestured dramatically towards her compatriot. "But I had to see you—I had to talk to you."

"Contessa. . . ." Not ungently, Signor Galleo placed a hand on her arm. "I had no wish to offend you. You are remarkable, you are incomparable, and I admire you as much as any man in Italy. But for this child. . . ." He stopped, and then went on talking in Italian. She answered him, rapidly and volubly, and as Candy stood staring a little dazedly from one to the other he suddenly seemed to give way.

"Very well, very well! Five minutes!" He looked across at Candy, and it seemed to her he looked desperately anxious. "Little one, whatever happens, don't be upset. Remember that to-night you are going to sing—nothing else happens!"

He went out, closing the door behind him, and for a moment the two women stood staring at one another. Then, to Candy's astonishment, huge, slow tears started to cascade down the Contessa's cheeks.

"Oh, Candida, Candida, I am sorry." Her voice sounded choked. "I know what it is like, a first night. And you have never appeared before! But—but, Michele...."

"Michele?" Candy's voice sounded small and still. "What about Michele?"

"You are close to him. What has he told you?"

"He hasn't told me anything, Contessa. I—I'm afraid you've got the wrong impression. Your son has helped me a lot, but I—we're not close friends." A little stiffly, she picked up the heavy, spreading skirts of her stage costume and moved across the room to pull a chair out for the visitor. "Won't you sit down?"

"You mean he hasn't told you about—why he went to Switzerland? You don't *know*?"

"Know?" Candy felt as if a chill ran through her, starting in the tips of her fingers and gradually spreading over her whole body. "I don't know anything—except that he went to Switzerland."

"But he has gone for an operation! He is ill—very ill—and, oh, Candy, I didn't know!"

"He ... he's ill?" Candy put out her right hand, and took hold of the back of a chair. The blood seemed to be pounding in her neck, and she felt as if reality were receding.

The Contessa sat down, and slowly, as if with difficulty, she told the English girl everything. A few months earlier Michele had developed a serious bone disease. He had seen all the foremost specialists in Rome and in London, but their verdict had been unanimous. At that point Candy looked at her with beseeching eyes.

"What was it—their verdict?" she whispered.

Anna Landi's lovely mouth trembled. "You must be brave, *cara*. They said . . . they said there was no hope for him. They gave him—eight or nine months. Perhaps more, but not . . . not long." She put a hand over her face, as if to shut out the world and everything in it. "I told you to be brave," she said in an odd, forced voice. "But I can't bear it, Candy! You must help me!"

"Why has he gone to Switzerland?" It seemed to Candy that her own voice came from a long way away.

"Because a few weeks ago he heard that in Switzerland there was a doctor who might be able to operate. There is not much chance of success, but there is—a very slight chance. It's—it's a very dangerous operation, Candy." Her voice rose hysterically. "Either it will be successful, or . . . or. . . ." She didn't need to finish.

"And you didn't know? You didn't know anything about it?" Candy spoke mechanically.

"Of course I didn't know. Marco was the only one who knew. I had no idea that he was even ill until Marco broke it to me this afternoon. Michele had written to him, asking him to tell me, now that he was going to—to have the operation, so that it wouldn't be too much of a shock, if—" She clasped her slim hands together. "Candy, I've been a terrible mother! To think that he couldn't tell me...."

"He couldn't tell you because he didn't want to upset you." Candy spoke gently. She felt as if she had risen above all ordinary feeling, and in some peculiar way her spirit had become detached from reality. "Surely you see that."

"But it's horrible! All these months...." The older woman stopped, gulping, and taking a handkerchief out of her bag began automatically to dab at her tear-streaked face. Then she looked at Candy as if something in the girl's face had caught her attention, and had startled her. After a long moment, she said huskily:

"It's as bad for you, isn't it?"

Candy stared back at her with eyes that made no attempt at any sort of concealment. "Yes," she said simply.

"Then you'll come with me ... you'll come with me to Switzerland, won't you?"

Before she could answer there was a knock on the door, and immediately afterwards it opened, and Signor Galleo walked in. His eyes went straight to Candy's face, and what he saw caused him to say something violent in Italian. Then he strode across the room, and put an arm around the shoulders of the slight figure in period costume as if he thought it might be necessary to protect her physically.

"My God! What is happening here?"

"Don't be angry, *signore*." Anna Landi stood up, and she suddenly looked what she was—a desperately unhappy middle-aged woman. "I know I should have waited until after the performance, but I couldn't—I couldn't do it." She walked towards Candy, and as, almost without meaning to do so, Lorenzo Galleo stood back, she put her arms around the English girl. "I know I was wrong, *cara*. It was cruel to tell you now. But it will not make any difference. All you must remember is that Michele is a good friend of yours, and one of his dearest wishes in the last few weeks has been to see you launched on the path that leads to becoming a great singer. If he can hear—if the news can reach him that you have had a big success to-night. . . ."

Unable to say any more, she kissed Candy on both cheeks, and then stood back and nodded to Lorenzo Galleo.

"I am going now. Candy, I'll see you afterwards?"

"Of course."

"My car will be waiting to take us to the airport."

"I see."

When she had gone, Signor Galleo closed the door behind her, and then glanced from his watch to Candy with obvious anxiety.

"My poor child, sit down. You have still ten minutes, but this is most unfortunate. What did she say to you? If it was bad news about young Michele I am truly sorry . . . truly sorry." He cleared his throat. "He is a friend of mine, and besides, of course. . . . Well, it's most unfortunate. But she doesn't mean to take you away after the performance?"

"Yes." Candy's lips felt stiff, but her voice was normal. "He's very ill . . . in Switzerland. The Contessa is going to see him. She—she wants me to go with her."

"You're in love with him?" The question was matter-of-fact.

Candy stood looking at the Italian as if she didn't really see him. Her face was inexpressibly sad. "That doesn't matter," she said at last. "I don't think anything matters very much."

"My dear—" He took a step towards her.

"Don't worry," she said steadily. "I'm not going to faint, or say I can't go on. I'm just going to do my best." She turned away to study her reflection in the mirror. "Do I—do I look all right?"

"You look wonderful," he told her truthfully. "*Incantevole*. But, Candy..." his eyes registered his uneasiness, "you are all right—really?"

"Absolutely all right." And she turned and smiled at him. Never, when she thought about it afterwards, was she ever able to understand how she managed that smile.

But she felt no nerves at all. Later, as she stood in the wings of the great theatre, waiting to go on stage, she felt as if she were standing outside herself, preparing to watch her own performance. It really did seem to her that nothing mattered—nothing, that was, except Michele. Michele, who instead of being here to-night to watch his efforts come to fruition was waiting in some Swiss clinic for an operation that would mean . . . that would mean—Abruptly, she checked herself. Michele was going to be all right—of course he was going to be all right. There was no other possibility.

Standing by herself, erect and graceful, her head thrown back and her eyes half closed, she felt the majesty of Gounod's music begin to creep into her soul, and the last shadows of doubt fled away from her.

She never did remember all the details of that evening. She did know that suddenly she was out on a wide stage, and an incredibly vast number of faces were looking up at her. They applauded her, warmly but not wildly at first, and then gradually their approval grew stronger. She slipped easily, almost naturally, into the role of Marguerite, the powerful tragedy of the story somehow appealing to her to-night. The magnitude of the part absorbed all her energies, demanded everything of which she was capable, and that total absorption was, more than anything, what she needed. She seemed to feel her voice gaining strength, her whole being gaining strength. Watching her from the wings, Lorenzo Galleo smiled.

She managed the Jewel Song with a competence and a lilting gaiety that drew almost a roar from the audience. Only one or two of those present had any idea just how poignant that gaiety was, but there were very few who didn't admire her skill . . . or who didn't appreciate that skill was only a very small part of what she was putting into her performance. She was inspired, throwing her heart and spirit into everything she sang, into her whole interpretation of the part, and the audience responded from the depths of its sensitive Italian being.

Then at last she was singing the final aria, and although she knew she was almost exhausted her voice soared with a new strength and clarity. The words she sang were alive with hope, with the triumph of good over evil, of light over darkness, and she felt as if they were lifting her up, giving her a magical new power that banished all her tension and weariness, and enabled her to bring her long ordeal to a conclusion in a way that drew the entire auditorium to its feet, and caused Lorenzo Galleo to draw a deep breath of relief and satisfaction.

The applause went on and on. Shouting and stamping and throwing flowers, the mass of people who had packed the old Florentine theatre to hear a new and untried English soprano demonstrated their enthusiasm in the way that was natural to them. And Candy, led out again and again and again for curtain-calls, gazed around at them in complete bewilderment. As flowers piled up about her feet she looked unbelieving, and after the first few minutes she began to feel almost panic-stricken. Why couldn't they let her go? She wanted to get away. . . . The noise was deafening and a little frightening.

During the tenth curtain-call a hot-house rosebud landed on her bare shoulder, and in her tense state she almost shrank back. Her eyes met the eyes of Signor Galleo, who had gone down into the front of the auditorium, and he nodded and disappeared. A minute or two later, when she once again found herself in the wings, he was there to meet her.

"*Brava, brava!*" Almost incandescent with enthusiasm, he lifted her hand and kissed it. "I knew it! I was sure. You were wonderful, incredible!"

She said nothing. In the background, the deafening roar of the audience went on. Lorenzo looked at her keenly, and a little anxiously.

"Yes, you have certainly had enough. I saw it from down there—it is why I came up. There will be no more curtain-calls. I will talk to them instead.

Gabriella!" He beckoned to one of the girls from the chorus. "Go with Signorina Wells to her dressing-room."

Candy found her voice just in time to call him back.

"Signor Galleo. . . ."

"Yes?" He came back to her immediately, his round dark eyes sparkling with a kind of paternal pride. "What is it?"

"I wanted to thank you. You've done such a lot for me. Thank you for helping me to get through all—all this."

"My child—" he began, but she interrupted him.

"And now I'll have to go." She got the words out quickly and firmly. "The Contessa will be waiting for me. As soon as I've changed—"

He looked at her long and earnestly. "Candy, are you sure? This is your night. It is an experience that will never come again. You should be here in Florence. The Principessa Vancini has planned a party for you. . . ."

"Then thank the Principessa for me, will you? Thank her very much." Her eyes were large and strained, but very serious. "Tell her I'd like to have gone to her party, but I was called away—urgently."

There was a short silence, and then he took her hands and pressed them. "*Bene*, my child, I understand. God go with you, and grant that you find good news at the end of your journey."

In her dressing-room she found the Contessa waiting for her, and with the skill and expertise of long experience the Italian woman helped her to change and get rid of her greasepaint. She had seen something of the performance, and she congratulated the girl warmly on her part in it, but her mind was a long way away, and it was obvious that she hadn't really taken very much of it in.

Lorenzo, acting quickly, had so organized things that all admirers and unwanted visitors were kept completely away from Candy's dressing-room, and when the time came for her and the Contessa to set out two doormen and Lorenzo himself were on hand to see them through the crush outside the stage door. The Contessa had turned up the high collar of her coat and put a scarf over her hair in an effort to conceal her own identity, but just as she reached the car, ahead of Candy, a reporter in the tightly-jammed press of people recognized her, and the crowd's interest in the two women doubled. It was almost a frightening moment, but somehow or other the doormen managed to get them safely into Anna's sleek, cream-coloured Citröen, and immediately the chauffeur drove off, as rapidly as he dared, through a tidal wave of running press photographers, into the old busy heart of Florence.

Just as they started off, something had been hurriedly pushed through the window by Lorenzo, but it wasn't until they were well on their way that Candy realized what it was. It was a bouquet of flowers—wonderful white roses—and automatically, without really thinking about it, she looked at the card that accompanied them. It was difficult to read, at first, for there was no light in the interior of the car, but in the glare of a passing street lamp she finally managed to make the words out. It said simply: *'Congratulations'*. And it was signed 'Michele'.

They stopped, briefly, at the Hotel Michelangelo, to pick up Candy's things, and then they were off again on their way to the airport. Candy, who was physically exhausted as well as worried and tense, talked very little, and her companion was just as silent. It wasn't until they were sitting in the departure lounge, waiting to board their plane for Geneva—the Contessa had booked both seats in advance—that either of them made any attempt to break the silence. It was Candy who finally did so. She had just thought of something.

"Caterina...." she said tentatively. "Does she—does she know about Michele?"

The Contessa was leaning back in her chair. Slowly she turned her elegant dark head and looked at Candy ... thoughtfully and a little anxiously.

"I thought you would have guessed," she said gently. "She has gone with him."

"Oh!" said Candy. "Of course...." Somehow, until just now, she had almost forgotten Caterina. But naturally she would be with Michele. He would want her more than anyone—more than anything on earth just now. Her own sole excuse for going was the fact that Michele's mother needed her. He would never know how much she, Candy, needed to be near him.

Their plane left just before midnight. With a handful of other passengers they walked out across the tarmac through a thin, cold drizzle, and by the time they got on board Candy's hair was damp, and she was grateful for the steady, comforting warmth of the cabin. She was not nervous of flying, and as the stewardesses temporarily stopped fussing round them, and the aircraft rose like a huge, throbbing bird into the distant, cloudy night sky she felt, for the first time that evening, as if some of the tension that filled her eased a little.

Whatever happened, she was on her way to Michele now. Every second that passed brought him nearer.

In her exhausted state the fantasy crept into her mind that if only she could reach him he would be all right. He *must* be all right. He must. . . . She struggled to keep awake, and for a time she managed it. But in the end her complete and utter emotional and physical weariness was something she could struggle against no longer.

By the time one of the stewardesses brought her the cup of coffee she had asked for she was fast asleep.

She awoke about two hours later to find that they were still airborne, and outside the windows the blackness of the February night was intense. Most of her fellow-passengers were fast asleep, but when she glanced sideways at Anna Landi's elegant profile she saw the long eyelashes quiver, and realized that although those spectacular dark eyes were completely hidden behind their carefully tinted lids their owner was definitely not asleep. A few seconds later, as if she had sensed that she was being watched, the Contessa opened her eyes and looked round.

"You're awake," she remarked.

"Yes," said Candy. She was beginning to wish she hadn't awakened so soon. The feeling of peace and relaxation that she had experienced just before she dropped off had vanished as if it had never been, and she felt cold and uneasy.

"Where is the clinic?" she asked. "Where Michele is?"

"Just over ten miles from Geneva. By the lake shore."

"Shall we be going straight there?"

"Yes. The operation is the day after to-morrow, so there isn't very much time."

Candy noticed that the older woman had lost all her tendency to be hysterical, and in its place a kind of cold, heavy sadness had dropped over her like a mantle.

On impulse, Candy said something that she had no real reason to believe was strictly true. "You know, I think he admires you a lot."

"Who? Michele?"

"Yes."

"No, my dear, he doesn't admire me. He despises me. For everything I have been, and for everything I have done, both to him and to his father."

"I don't understand."

"No? Well, I will explain it to you. At times like this one can tell things that...that normally one would never mention." She made herself more comfortable in her seat, and lifted one of her hands to study the blaze of rings that weighed it down. "I was married when I was very young...just seventeen. I was already becoming a successful film actress—in Italy," a little wryly, "we sometimes begin our careers very early in life. But then the rich Conte di Lucca wanted to marry me, and I thought 'I shall be a great lady. I shall have a *palazzo* in Rome, and a *villino* near Genoa, and everyone will respect me.' So I married him...and two years later I had Michele." Her voice grew rather harsh. "But I never loved my husband, and for a long time I didn't think I even loved his child."

"Did you...love anyone?" Candy asked gently.

"Yes. I loved Marco, my husband's brother. And he

loved me. He never forgave me for marrying Giovanni —that was my husband's name. And later, too, he came to hate me for what I became—a self-centred woman without a thought for either my husband or my child. As you know, he has never married, and when I feel a need to comfort myself I say that it is because he could not love anyone but me. But really—really I know it is because I showed him what a woman could become."

Candy said nothing. So that was the truth about Marco di Lucca! That was the story behind his restless, unhappy life! The Contessa was speaking again.

"Even when he came to me, yesterday, to break the news to me that Michele was ill, I knew he had not forgiven me. I don't suppose he ever will. I—" She broke off, her voice unsteady.

Candy looked at her, and understood something. The fabulous Anna Landi, the Contessa di Lucca—the famous beauty who surrounded herself with more admiring men than almost any other woman in the glittering international set in which she moved—was after all these years still in love with her brother-in-law . . . the jaded, disillusioned Marco di Lucca.

She understood, now, that men like John Ryland were, as far as the Contessa was concerned, only the merest passing whim. She didn't think the Contessa knew that there had ever been anything serious between herself and John, and it didn't matter now.

It was still quite dark when they arrived in Geneva, and as they left the aircraft and made their way down the gangway the sharp, bitter cold of Switzerland in February came to meet them. They passed without difficulty through Customs and Immigration control, and then they waited just inside the airport's main doors while their luggage was carried out to a taxi.

But they hadn't been waiting for long before a voice hailed them; a sleepy, familiar Italian voice. And Anna started and swung round with an eagerness that was entirely revealing.

"Marco!" He had just come in through the glass doors, and she went forward a little to meet him. "Marco, how did you get here?"

"By aeroplane, Anna, just as you did—only a few hours earlier." He looked at Candy. "Good morning, little one." Then his face grew grave. "You sang last night? You did not cancel the performance?"

"No. She sang," Anna answered for her. "She sang like an angel. But she left immediately afterwards, to come here with me."

"I tried to get to Florence ahead of you last night," he admitted ruefully. "I wanted to speak to Candy before you did—to make sure that she went ahead as Michele wished her to."

"Then why did you not arrive?" Anna demanded, just a little sharply.

"My car broke down less than twenty kilometres north of Rome. So I decided to fly on to Switzerland, in order to be here ahead of you."

His voice was cold and unemotional, almost flippant. But, although it was only visible for a moment, Candy didn't miss the look that hovered in his eyes as they rested on the lovely face of his sister-in-law.

As it was still only four o'clock in the morning, and also they did have quite a bit of luggage with them, they didn't go straight to the clinic after all, but instead instructed their taxi-driver to convey them to a well-known lakeside hotel a short distance away from it. There they refreshed themselves after their journey by washing and changing, and both Marco and the Contessa did everything in their power to persuade Candy to go to bed.

"I will see that you are awakened, *carina,* if there is anything to hear—anything at all," Anna assured her gently. "You are exhausted, and must have rest."

"But I don't want to sleep," Candy protested. "I—I'm not tired." And then it occurred to her that perhaps, after all, they would be glad to have her out of the way for a while. It was true that Anna had asked for her company, but this whole thing was, after all, an essentially private family concern, and she was an outsider. "I won't worry you" she promised anxiously. "I'll go for a walk, or something. . . ."

The Contessa shook her head at her. "Oh, Candy, don't be silly."

She was alone in her room when the sun came up. Standing by her window, she saw the vast darkness of the lake outside turn slowly to silver, and the tops of the surrounding mountains to gold. She had visited Switzerland once before, during her schooldays, and its beauty had amazed her then, as it did now. But this morning it seemed to her that it was a cold, curiously empty beauty, and it gave her no comfort.

Immediately after an early breakfast, they all set off by taxi for the clinic. The drive along by the lakeshore was spectacular, and under any other circumstances Candy would have appreciated it to the full, but since her arrival in Switzerland the whole terrible reality of what was happening had descended on her with the force of a physical weight, and her heart felt like stone. She couldn't feel hope or confidence, now—she couldn't feel anything except a despair as grey and unfathomable as those wide areas of the lake in front of her that had not yet been touched by the sun.

The clinic was a spreading, white-walled building surrounded by neat, English-style lawns and thickets of silver birch trees. For a medical institution it was certainly outstandingly attractive, and Candy had to admit to herself that at sight of it her heart did lift a little. Perhaps in this lovely setting ... Swiss doctors were supposed to be very clever, after all. Perhaps ... ? She didn't dare to carry her thinking to its logical conclusion.

They were received by the staff with interest, and a certain amount of respect. The Conte di Lucca had had a good night, and was quite well this morning. The operation was planned for to-morrow. In the meantime. ...

Very soon Anna and her brother-in-law had been whisked upstairs for consultations with a senior specialist, and Candy, left alone, wandered through the gardens. At first she wondered why it was that there were absolutely no flowers, and then she remembered that it was February. Of course there were no flowers. She thought of her white roses, now reposing in a vase in her hotel bedroom, and her eyes filled with tears.

Oh, Michele. ...

It seemed a very long time later that the others rejoined her, and when they did it was obvious that Anna had been crying. But she smiled at Candy.

"Go up and see him, *cara*. He is asking for you. They will take you up."

Inside the quiet, sun-filled building, with a tranquil, uniformed nursing Sister in a starched coif escorting her up in a lift and then along what seemed like miles of corridor to a distant wing, she felt as if her nerves were about to give out completely. She had never expected him to send for her—she didn't know why, but it hadn't at any time occurred to her that he could want to see an outsider like herself.

The room that had been allotted to Michele was undoubtedly one of the best the establishment had to offer, and when Candy first hesitantly followed the nurse through the doorway she was almost blinded by the brilliance of the morning light pouring in through the wide picture windows. At first glance it was all much more strongly reminiscent of a luxury hotel than a clinic; but then her eyes took in the neat, narrow, hospital-style bed, with its attendant charts and shining equipment, and something seemed to turn over in the region of her heart.

The bed had been made up, and there was nothing, as far as Candy could see, to indicate the presence of a patient, but the nurse smiled, and gestured towards the balcony.

"He is out there, *mademoiselle*." And then she effaced herself, and Candy was left to make her way out on to the balcony alone.

He was sitting in a large basket-work chair, staring out across the magnificent panorama of lake and mountain that was spread in front of him like a theatre backcloth, and when Candy first caught sight of him she was conscious of a little upsurge of relief because he looked so normal—so completely himself. She wasn't sure what sort of changes she had expected an interval of a few days to have brought about in him, but she knew she had expected something. And yet there he was, looking just as he had looked on that evening last October, when she had opened the door of the drawing-room at Great Mincham, and he had been there, playing the piano.

She understood, now, that look in his eyes that had so puzzled her—the melancholy detachment that must have had its roots in despair.

She moved so quietly that for a moment or two he didn't realize she was there. And then he looked up, and the expression on his face startled her, setting every pulse she possessed throbbing wildly.

"Candida!" He stood up.

"How—how are you?" she asked lamely.

He didn't answer, but simply went on looking at her in a way that almost bewildered her. "Candida," he said at last, "I didn't mean you to come here."

Desperately uncertain, not knowing what to say, she murmured: "The Contessa asked me to come. To—to keep her company."

His voice and expression changed a little. "Yes. . . . Of course." He indicated a chair close beside his own, and she sat down rather thankfully.

"Well, how was it . . . last night? My mother tells me you had a great success."

"It's very kind of her to say so. I think it did go rather well."

"I wish I could have been there." His voice was gentle.

She wanted to say: "So do I," but even if she had had the nerve to do so the words wouldn't have come.

He was talking about Caterina. "She was sorry, too, that she could not be there . . . very sorry. But she came with me because—"

"Yes, of course—I know." How could he suppose she didn't understand that Caterina, who was to be his wife, had had to go with him?

"I would have postponed. . . ." he was saying slowly. "But the doctors told me there was no more time. You understand, don't you?"

"Yes," she said, and thought the monosyllable had never sounded more hopelessly inadequate. She felt almost like screaming. If only he would stop talking about her own wretched, miserable singing debut as if it were important . . . when the only thing that mattered in the whole wide world was that his operation should be a success, his recovery complete. Desperately, she looked away from him, and as she stared out across the smooth surface of the shining lake she knew that if she were only to be given the chance she would give up every hope for her own future . . . if by doing so she could help him. The fact that he didn't love her made no difference whatsoever. If he came through the operation he would almost certainly marry Caterina, but she didn't care. At least, she did care . . . she cared terribly, but her caring wasn't important.

The only thing that was important was that he should be all right—that, after to-morrow, his road ahead should be clear and bright. That after to-morrow there should be a road ahead.

"Candida," he said suddenly, "look at me!"

She obeyed, her pale cheeks flushing faintly.

"Tell me...." He was watching her so intently that she felt the colour grow deeper. "Last night you had a great success. It has made you very happy?"

"Happy?" Her eyes revealed her bewilderment.

"Yes. It was what you wanted, wasn't it?"

"I...." She turned her head away. "Yes, of course."

"Then I have achieved what I set out to achieve."

Her throat contracted; she dared not speak, and in near desperation she stood up.

"Candy...." It was the first time that he had used the shortened form of her name. "You're not going, Candy?"

"I mustn't tire you," she managed stiffly.

"You won't tire me. I don't feel ill, and my condition cannot be *made* worse. It's not that sort of an illness."

"Yes, but—"

"I don't want you to go, Candy. Not yet."

He had risen to his feet, and was standing behind her. She felt his breath stirring her hair, and her pulses began to race.

"If—if everything goes well you will come and see me again, won't you? After the operation? You can stay until then?"

"If you want me to," a little unsteadily. "But you'll have Caterina."

"Caterina?" He sounded surprised.

"Well, she'll be staying on, won't she?"

"Not for long. She begins her novitiate at the Convent of the Holy Angels on the tenth of this month."

Candy swung round to face him. "Her... what did you say?" she asked in a small voice.

"Her novitiate. Hasn't she told you? She finally made up her mind only two or three days ago, but the idea has been with her since she was a child. She is definitely to become a nun."

"A... nun?"

"Yes. But why are we talking about Caterina?"

She wasn't thinking clearly enough to dissemble. "I—I thought you were going to marry her."

For several seconds there was silence, while he stared down into her face. Then he spoke, softly and huskily. "You thought I was going to marry Caterina?"

"Yes." She was afraid to look at him.

"But... Candy, Caterina and I have been close friends since we were children. That is why she came here with me, and why she will wait—at least until to-morrow before going back to Rome. But we have never been anything but friends. During the last few months she has slowly been coming to a decision about her vocation, and because she and I are like brother and sister we have spent a great deal of time discussing it together. It has been a difficult time for her. She needed to tell her thoughts to someone. But there has never been anything more than that between us."

So that was it! It accounted for everything—even the time Caterina and Michele had spent together on Christmas night. For the simple reason that she couldn't do anything to prevent it, her lower lip started to tremble, and without looking up she knew that Michele had noticed.

And then she was in his arms, and he was holding her so tightly that she couldn't breathe. Tears cascaded down her cheeks, and she hid her face against him.

"Oh, Candy . . . *carina*!" His sensitive fingers stroked her hair unsteadily. "I was so afraid—so afraid you didn't want me! I thought you only wanted your music. That was what I wanted for you at first—I had seen how Ryland had made you suffer, and I vowed to myself that I would teach you to live for your heavenly voice—to spread your wings and soar out of reach of everything that could bring a cloud into your eyes. But it was no good—I fell so desperately in love with you!"

Dizzy and unbelieving, she looked up, and as he bent his head and kissed her the world was dissolved in light, and a peace such as she had never dreamed of enveloped her like a mantle. "I love you," she whispered. "Oh, Michele, I love you more than anything on earth—more than life! Music means nothing to me by comparison with you."

He laid his cheek against her hair, and when he spoke his voice quivered with remorse.

"I didn't mean to say anything until . . . unless. . . ." It wasn't necessary for him to finish.

"Oh, darling!" She lifted her eyes to his, and although in their depths there was anguish there was also a brilliant, glowing light. "I'm so glad you did."

They were silent for what seemed a very long time. And then at last he lifted his head and looked down at her.

"Candy, you know that during the next twenty-four

185

hours everything will be—well, in the hands of God."

She nodded.

"It is just that I worry about you. If—if anything should happen . . . if the future doesn't work out for us. . . ."

"Don't," she whispered. "Don't say that. Everything is going to be all right—I know it is. But even if. . . . Michele, some time, somewhere, we'll be together. Whatever happens."

And as he bent and kissed her hair he knew that she was right. For them there would never be any parting.

CHAPTER TEN

THE operation was scheduled to begin at ten a.m. the
following day, and just before that time Candy and the
Contessa di Lucca, together with Marco, arrived at the
clinic. Candy was very pale, but absolutely calm. Nobody had asked her any questions about what had
happened between her and Michele the previous
morning, but everybody had guessed without the
smallest difficulty, and had been exceptionally gentle
with her ever since.

At the clinic they met Caterina, whom they had also
seen the previous afternoon, and as Candy kissed her
she felt all over again the overwhelming wonder she had
felt when she first heard the truth about the relationship
between the other girl and Michele. Without revealing
anything else, she let Caterina know that she had been
told about her plans, and they talked for a long time.
The conversation acted as a sort of opiate, through
which Candy felt the anguish of icy fear hovering about
her all the time, striving to take her over, body and
soul.

The authorities at the clinic didn't seem to think it in
the least odd that no fewer than four close relatives and
friends should wish to wait on the premises for news of
the Conte di Lucca, and they were allotted a pleasant
private sitting-room overlooking not the mountains but
the tranquil woods and gardens behind the building.

Candy noticed that for most of the time Anna and her brother-in-law sat close together, and it was obvious that at last the gulf between them had been bridged. For Anna the presence of Marco was the source of all comfort, and for Marco. ... Candy watched him with fascination as, his face transformed by solicitude—and something much stronger than solicitude—he hovered protectively about the woman he had loved for so long.

Anna had told her that everything had been put right, too, between herself and Michele, and for that Candy was profoundly grateful.

Slowly the minutes dragged by and became hours. Coffee was served to them and then more coffee, but Candy didn't drink any of it. She had faith—she knew she had faith, and every so often she closed her eyes and tried to shut everything but that faith out of her mind, but still the icy fingers of fear reached out and clasped at her heart, and she was obsessed by a feeling that she was walking the edge of a high precipice. When she tried to speak her voice and throat were dry, and when she tried to move her whole body felt stiff. It was understandable, she told herself. It wasn't only Michele's life that hung in the balance : it was her own as well.

All at once, after what seemed like an eternity of silence, Caterina spoke to her.

"Did you know," she asked softly, "that when Michele first met you he had just seen the London specialist who gave him no hope?"

Candy shook her head.

"Well, it's true. That day was a black one for him. He has told me he felt surrounded by darkness. But then he met you, and he says you became for him a ray of light in the darkness."

"Oh!" It was a quivering whisper.

"At first he wished only to help you sing. So he arranged everything . . . your coming to Rome, Signor Galleo—everything. Whatever story they told you about it was not true. Michele did it all." She stopped. "I tell you," she said quietly, "because I know it will make you happy, not ashamed."

Candy's eyes glowed. So she owed everything to him! He was behind everything in her life that had any value.

"Yes," she said after a pause, "it makes me very happy."

Ten minutes later, at exactly twenty-seven minutes past one, the door opened and the senior specialist whom Anna and Marco had seen the day before appeared on the threshold. He was looking at Anna.

"Madame," he said quietly, "may I speak with you?"

The Contessa stood up slowly. Her eyes were terrible. Marco di Lucca accompanied her to the door, and they both went out with the doctor.

Candy, unable to say anything, turned her head to look at the older girl beside her. Caterina, her face a mask of serenity, was whispering a prayer, and even in that moment Candy was conscious of a profound admiration for an unusual and dedicated spirit.

In after years she never did know how long they waited for somebody to come back and join them in the quiet room, but it seemed like ten years. A dreadful conviction had her in its grip, a conviction that she couldn't shake off, and by the time the door opened again her hands were wet with perspiration, her whole body chilled.

It was Anna who opened the door, and she looked straight across at Candy.

"*Cara*," she said in an odd voice, "you must hurry upstairs. Don't keep him waiting. He is asking for you!"

The white-walled, grey-carpeted room with its picture windows was still sunlit, still reminiscent of something in a luxury hotel. But this time Candy didn't even notice.

The only things she saw were a narrow, clinical bed, and a figure whose warm brown eyes lit like lamps at the sight of her. Scarcely able to see for the mist in front of her eyes, she dropped to her knees beside the bed, and one of Michele's hands came out to clasp hers with amazing strength.

"*Carina*," he murmured. "There are no more clouds!"

"No, darling." Still crying, she pressed her lips to the back of his hand.

He looked at her as if she were the most wonderful thing he would ever hope to see on earth. "There's a song in your eyes," he said slowly. "All this time, I've felt that you were singing above the clouds."

She gave him a smile that was like sunlight. And she knew that for the rest of their lives as long as she could be with him, something inside her would always be singing.

A Treasury of Harlequin Romances!

Many of the all time favorite Harlequin Romance Novels have not been available, until now, since the original printing. But on this special introductory offer, they are yours in an exquisitely bound, rich gold hardcover with royal blue imprint. Three complete unabridged novels in each volume. And the cost is so very low you'll be amazed!

This very special collection of classic Harlequin Romances would be a distinctive addition to your library. And imagine what a delightful gift they'd make for any Harlequin reader!

Start your collection now. See reverse of this page for **SPECIAL INTRODUCTORY OFFER!**

v